A little
HUNGARIAN
pornography

A LITTLE HUNGARIAN PORNOGRAPHY

PÉTER ESTERHÁZY

TRANSLATED BY JUDITH SOLLOSY

hydra
books

NORTHWESTERN UNIVERSITY PRESS

EVANSTON, ILLINOIS

Hydra Books
Northwestern University Press
Evanston, Illinois 60208-4210

Printed in the United States of America

ISBN 0-8101-1577-8

Library of Congress Cataloging-in-Publication Data

Esterházy, Péter, 1950–
    [Kis magyar pornográfia. English]
    A little Hungarian pornography / Péter Esterházy ; translated by Judith Sollosy.
        p. cm.
    ISBN 0-8101-1577-8
    I. Title.
PH3241.E85K513 1995
894'.51133—dc20

                                                                95-25048
                                                                CIP

The paper used in this publication meets the minimum requirements of the American National Standard for Information Sciences—Permanence of Paper for Printed Library Materials, ANSI Z39.48-1984.

Preface

Life in a dictatorship is not the same as life in a democracy. You live in a different way. And you write in a different way, too. You also read in a different way. And though literary considerations everywhere are equally 'lasting as steel', literature is nevertheless affected by the just-mentioned difference. Some books are irrevocably the prisoners of the time in which they were written. The author hopes (not that he's got a choice) that his book is perhaps an exception, that time has not done too much damage. Of course, all sorts of shackles and loose bindings flapping this way and that are in evidence throughout its pages, which, to say the least, have their own special logic.

This is the author's most East-European book, and his most helpless, too. It was written in 1982–3, in the overripe period of the Kádár era, under small, Hungarian, pornographic circumstances where pornography should be understood as meaning lies, the lies of the body, the lies of the soul, our lies. Let us imagine, if we can, a country where everything is a lie, where the lack of democracy is called socialist democracy, economic chaos socialist economy, revolution anti-revolution, and so on.

The dictatorship of the time was a real dictatorship, though it was neither bloody nor crude. For all practical purposes, it meant the potential threat of dictatorship, a ubiquitous and unavoidable threat that tainted every moment of our lives. *If*, you thought to yourself, *if it should happen*. And you felt helpless. But usually there was no *if*. *It* did not happen.

Such a total, all-encompassing lie, when from history through green-pea soup, when from our father's eyebrows and our lover's lap everything is a lie, not to mention this theoretical yet very tangible presence of threat, all this makes for a highly poetic situation. The language of the real dictatorship of the fifties was silence, keeping mum. That of the seventies and the eighties was the avoidance of speech, not talking about *it*. The time was not yet ripe to speak out 'properly'. But you could at least *hint* that you could not speak out properly. Under the circumstances, the literature of the period automatically took advantage of the aesthetic possibility suggested by a constant cramp in one's stomach. It took advantage of the elemental terror that certain words hold (Stalin, Rákosi, ÁVÓ). It used terror as an aesthetic creative force.

This book was written during a so-called time of transition (though who has ever heard of a time that was not transitional?) when Hungarian literature (or part of it at least) was fed up to here with this encoded, oblique, reading-between-the-lines type of writing and collusion, and rejected the help coming from the cramp in the stomach, all the while taking advantage of it, inadvertently of course.

Putting an end to this bad situation should have been the business of the readers and not the writers. It should have been something for society to attend to. But at the time, the readers (for reasons of their own) did not yet want to chase the Russians out of Hungary.

Whether in the end it was the Hungarians who chased the Russians out or not is debatable. But leave they did. And with that, some of the political edge of the book, if ever there was any, was blunted. The author nevertheless relies on the circumstance that all countries everywhere will surely have small Hungarian-type pornographic stories of their own.

Péter Esterházy

CONTENTS

The Trabant grips the road
exceptionally well. Its acceleration
is first-rate. This, however,
must not encourage reckless
and irresponsible driving.

(from the Trabant's instruction manual)

I

(on the back seat of a Pobyeda)

> *I looked forward to the evening*
> *because I love Slovak women, and*
> *for a handful of reasons prefer them*
> *to Czech women: first, because they*
> *have more style, second, because*
> *they are less emancipated, and*
> *third, because at that certain moment*
> *they cry OY!*
> *(Milan Kundera: The Messenger)*

'Your drink, sir, it is for you! Ebony eyes, a moist, red poppy, black hair, the luscious, dark brown of the begonias. She stands at the panoramic window laughing impishly. Behind her the palm leaves tremble in the breeze. A snow-white grey heron or egret (?!) lolls on a trembling banana leaf. In the distance the white-crested waves crash against the coral reefs. There is no clock to tick away the time but now and then a slothful coconut comes tumbling to the ground. The little frencher! Good thing she didn't bite off a piece while she was at it! The tempo: take it slow, take it slow, good Master Rákóczi[1] and she does her pleasure as if her gullet were her clitoris.

---

[1] The tempo is the same as the folk song from which the fragment comes. Ferenc Rákóczi II (1645–76) was leader of the Kurucz forces fighting the Habsburgs in the insurrection that bears his name. Although they produced some impressive partial results, they ended, as always, in Habsburg victory.

'Were you perhaps indisposed yesterday?' the department head asked, turning to the pretty secretary he had set his sights on for trade union trustee. But his tone of voice betrayed the lack of trust that became every communist's second nature during the Hard Times.

The little miss with the wiggly behind gave an awkward smile. 'Yes, Comrade Department Head. And the doctor got me in bed right away.'

'But that was reason for *you* to have taken the entire day off right away!'

Once upon a time there lived a cop, and once this cop, for reasons that must here remain obscure, kissed his stick. Your first reaction may be one of disbelief: What?! What's this I hear?! The protector of the peace that is *ours*?

Well, why not? would be our unhurried *sechas* counter-question. Because, let's face it. Our illustrious police force is neither an agglomeration nor a reservoir of individuals who are *incomplete*. No, sirree! For what sort of work is it after all? Heroic, doubtless. But also time-consuming and perilous. Little wonder if it attracts a disproportionate number of bachelors and maidens fair.

What choice is there, then, except to go in search, through thick and thin, of a convenient occasion, though not (need we stress?) by violating work regulations! Which holds out the hope, at least, of finding one's psychological balance along with a natural attitude to life, not to mention the elemental aspects of love. Anyone who has ever been accosted in this homeland of ours by a morose, irritable and frustrated policeman knows how that ain't nothin', and that ain't nothin'!

'I don't know what to do. My wife wants to have our baby scraped out by common consent.' *Conversely*: on a state-operated package tour to Bangkok a 19-year-old dancer said to a friend of mine, a likeable teddy-bear of a man, *You are big.*

'Wait, my friend, *s'il vous plaît*,' I said to the gloomy young man who reminded me so much of my own former self just before graduation. I would have liked to ask him what final exam questions he had been given, but I asked him only about the preparations instead – would he kindly 'arrange a little *liberation there*'. 'Guess what. I got to talk about the poetry of the *Nyugat*! No kidding! The *West*!'[2] 'Fear not, little cousin, it's probably just a touch of organic dysfunction, happily a less complicated business than the dysfunction of the soul!' 'Help me, please,' the boy said, his voice pained. *'After all, you are the engineer of the soul and you do love yourself so!'*

What can one say to that? What is thinkable is also possible. 'Let's wait and *see*.'

And truly, when I attempted to pull back the foreskin rising into

[2] The *Nyugat*: the literary journal founded in 1908 and considered the cradle of modern Hungarian letters. Everyone started from it or ended with it, or else took it as an affront. When discussing 20th-century Hungarian literature, there is talk of the first, second, third (and *n*-th) generation of the *Nyugat*. Of the authors in the book, Mihály Babits, Zsigmond Móricz, Géza Csáth, Gyula Illyés and György Rónay all belonged to one *Nyugat* generation or another. In the fifties, the *Nyugat* was a despised example of literature for its own sake. 'Writers with a quality-fetish,' Minister of Culture Révai called its champions.

a point over the glans, it was not possible, for it was stuck. In Lit Crit I had to talk about Móricz's short stories.[3] Went like a breeze. *I luv More Ritz* (sign on a tee shirt). I said as much to the boy, by way of comfort. But did he catch on in his all too human flurry of emotion, I wonder? . . .

Which reminds me. The question, what is a writer supposed to be doing around these parts has produced answers stranger than fiction, though they were not *necessarily* born of feeble-mindedness. They were born of misery, the misery of the situation, which does not make them any different from what they are. But they've got a reason, at least. Which is what we call misery. Through the years, the task has been formulated basically in relationship to the necessity of *regulating* the River Tisza, making it fit for navigation, and thus making the nation *prosper*, whereas there is something very wrong *to begin with* if the Tisza needs to be regulated by other than experts, while the nation – well, the nation had better be left to fend for itself with (need we add?) the wiser than wise counsel of its honourable and highly qualified leaders. All other eventualities can only be worse. It is more comforting if the writer thinks not in terms of *the* people and *the* homeland, but in terms of subject and predicate, and not because he is a homeless villain, but because if he's any good at all, he's *up to here* in it anyhow, and if he's no good, what's the use of *talking*? He's just mincing his words. Love of country is a matter of quality.

[3] *A Concise History of Hungarian Literature* calls Zsigmond Móricz (1879–1942) 'the greatest prose writer, unsurpassed to this day'. Despite this fact, he really is a great prose writer – and a critical eye if ever there was one for 'the moral decadence of the bourgeoisie'.

But where was I? Oh yes. Grabbing a pair of sterilised scissors I cut an inch-length incision in the foreskin so the glans could lie unhampered. However, as I had expected, this did not do the trick. With the utmost care I separated the fine, silky mucous membrane from the lower corona ridge, whereupon I could begin the actual incision for which I pulled the foreskin, by now mobile, towards the tip, but only so I could quickly stretch it out with a surgical clamp. Then, dispensing with the extra piece of skin, I sutured up the lesion with small, expert stitches.

'*The object is simple*,' I said craftily by way of self-criticism.

I am a writer. I go for red wine, flashy cars, thick steaks, fast women and nature (most especially grass and the daddy-longlegs) in a big way, and I like to sleep till seven-thirty at least, because I deserve it. Accordingly, seeing how it began with a phone call which came well before seven a.m., our little chronicle brought with it its fair share of burden.

On the perilous, barbed-wire no man's land between dreaming and waking it dawned on me only by degrees that the early morning caller was Klára, of whom I have many pleasant memories. I wished her in hell. (She was the kind of girl who wouldn't say at such and such a time, or Monday, for instance, or in March, for instance, or in '72, for instance, but 'at the time *I had my difficulties* with Baudelaire'. Which did precious little to facilitate the flow of our discourse. It happened a long, long time ago; perhaps it didn't even happen at all.) Stealthily, we agreed on a quickie.

The enervated sunlight waltzed extravagantly around the room. We were a little uptight. We knew each other, yet we knew each other not. Just a bit stiff, I asked her to take a comfortable seat on my sofa. She willingly obliged.

'Well, what is it?' I asked her after her difficulties. 'It is so embarrassing,' she said, gently squirming. Her breasts were still – the way they were. Then she sighed profusely and bent into it.

'Last year my husband cheated on me with a woman from the office. *He laid her on his desk and took possession of her.* He first put down the stapler and folders, though. He has a very respon-sible job.' It was quiet. They were building a workers' hostel next door. They're going to be veritable little *suites*, I'm told. Oh, how I love their cranes! And the fact they're *building* like this. 'He is practically a *slave* to that woman!'

Irked, I broke into her, slave, slave, slave! The way we throw words around! Especially those of us who are being cheated on . . . It's not easy, being a slave. More often than not, the problem lies hidden someplace else.

'Do not misconstrue me, I implore you! You are right! We suffer difficulties in the sphere of physical bliss. Which is why he's seeing that *cocotte*.' I thought of a friend of mine. We used to sit in the kitchen for hours, cleaning potatoes. There was nothing else, just the sound of the potato skin. We fed her kids, then placed our fingers in each other's genitals. 'God loves you.' I said nothing. Then, flinging caution to the wind, Klára began to sob. 'My husband is himself undecided. He says he loves me, and he's telling the truth, I know he is! The other day, too, he comes bolting out of the john and *without prior notice* says how while he was pissing, holding his dick, *it hit him*, he loves me. It's not something you can make up just like that . . . Except sometimes he drags that other woman here to our nuptial chamber and then I have to sleep with the kids. We play "he who laughs last laughs best". All night. They don't know what to make of it, of course, even if they usually win, what I mean is, end up laughing in the end . . . We did it all together, the house too.'

'How old is your husband?' 'Fifty-two.' 'I see,' I said thoughtfully with all the gracious slyness of my thirty-two years, as if I were twenty-two. We paused briefly and I watched expectantly, feeling – it is part of my profession! – that this was not the whole truth. And wouldn't you know, she finally blurted it out.

'My husband says it's loose. That he often has the feeling he can't be making me properly happy, that, *metaphorically speaking*, it feels like a musician playing in a concert hall too big for his purposes. And that the other's is wholly different down there, which is much more to his liking, and that's why he can't *come*, try as he might, even though he is *convinced* I am of more *worth*.' She even cried over this contradiction, poor thing.

Like a heavy cloud of mist did hope hover above the woman's features. Yet aren't we all like this, friends? I was desperate. There has to be a solution! It's not right that smart young people of *worth*, bent on action, should be thus condemned! It's not what our forebears fought for, it's not what we are fighting for, no sirree!

'Here it comes!' I screamed, trembling from the full force of the impact. After so much time, there we were, trembling in sweet unison. 'The muscles. They need tightening.' 'Tightening,' Klára repeated dumbly. I nodded, for a woman's cooch, like a fortifi-

cation by soldiers or a honeycomb by bees, is circled all around
by muscles.

Concentration had distorted Klára's face. Mourning has the same
effect on the face of a friend of mine. We attended a funeral
once, which is how I know. His forehead narrowed, *everything
out of proportion*, his eyes moving unintelligently closer, and the
fact that they were crossed didn't help matters any. Yet if grief
could be measured, surely mine was the greater. But it can't. Of
course, I have no idea what my own face looked like at the
time . . .

'Relax and let yourself go, no clothes, then introduce a finger of
your choice half-way or more into the holy of holies. Right at
the entrance, where in another place you'd expect to find the
holy water stoop, you'll find a sphincter muscle. When you cough,
for instance, it contracts. Moving it at will is what you must learn
to do.' 'Is that all?' she asked incredulously. I patted her cute
little cheeks.

'No.'

(I might as well stop here, though. I explained to her in detail
about the levator, the subsequent soreness, and that sort of thing.)

'You want me to think about that *all the time*? That's awful! To
always have to . . . without ever being able to . . . and not a
moment's . . .' Laughing, I shook my head. 'Don't worry. It'll
come of its own accord. The climax of your joy shall squeak in
seven languages! You'll take to it, we all have, like a puppy dog
to its barking.'

Dazed and hopeful, she rose from my sofa and made for the bathroom. But she spun round and giving a merry little cough said [*self-censored*]! What the picture represents is its sense.

My next-door neighbour, the woman next door, always looks bashful, anxious and virginally modest despite her thirty-two years. When we meet she blushingly lowers her eyes towards the nether regions, that's how timid she is. But she is graceful, too, a stunner with golden hair and a shape like a doll's.

At the time I was locked in hand-to-hand combat with the sparrow-hawk dreams of my private life, not being able to choose between two women, sometimes cheating on the one, sometimes the other – and invariably on myself. The woman next door used to help me out by way of sugar or mayonnaise and anxious, I reciprocated with books. Once I gave her a short story anthology, adding that it was put out by Magvető, the Seed Sower. She seemed to take the hint. As for her shyness, I hoped she'd lose it, leaning soberly against my rococo sofa.

And so it transpired. She promptly *let go*. 'It's much better now,' she herself admitted. 'What we stand to lose when we are over-excited is the thing that got us overexcited in the first place,' I ventured, feeling like a murderer being hoist on his own petard, assuming, of course, I *was* a murderer. I pulled myself back into reality, into the realistically existing real, and called the woman's attention to the sphere of jurisdiction which belongs to art and that help was to be expected, if at all, from a detailed and conscientious report furnished by her, but she mustn't for a moment think she'll be *exposing* herself thereby. Our job is to put our nose to the grindstone and take an in-depth look at *reality*.

'My dreams,' she began. I burst out laughing. It was meant to be derisive, but it eluded her. 'Our dreams! My dear little fool, what do you want with our dreams!' But I was on the wrong trail. 'In my dreams my dreams are beautiful, though by morning they are odious and ugly.' Her voice had a resolute ring to it. '*Pro forma* it is highly embarrassing that as a mother and married woman I should be dreaming about being a naked dancer with a string of conquests to my credit . . . The dream is I am happy because my husband and I, we go all out, but then I suddenly let go of the reins and, hips gyrating, I find myself standing before the public. I shower strange men with innuendoes and insinuations of a private nature accompanied by lewd movements.

'The band, the boys! playing exotic, dark music. It's hot, hot! My husband's gone, and my ass is hot! I can *feel* . . . Leisurely, I unbutton my blouse, and with a twirling, whirling motion, my skirt, too, falls like a whirlwind around my ankles. The marked slenderness of my thighs fills me with pleasure, the school-boy slenderness of my hips, too. They are not going to tell on me. Only a bra and a tiny pair of panties cover the ultimate riddle now. There is expectant silence. The band, too, has forgotten to play. Then I see it's the foursome from the office, the director, the chief engineer, the Party secretary and the trade union trustee. Which of course just adds fuel to my fire.

'The ones in the back stand on chairs so as not to miss anything, and I don't blame them. I am *here*, I'm okay, I go for myself in a really big way. My husband stands, too; I face him as I strip off my bra, drop dead, you fart! I am rewarded by an effusion of appreciative applause . . . When my panties are gone, I wake up, always, my nightie bunched up into a fist-size ball between my burning thighs. As you'd expect, my husband is sleeping, of course.'

I took her blushing cheeks between my hands and called her attention to the fact that she's got nothing to be ashamed of, in the appreciation of those strangers she is only seeking to fill the void, a result of her husband's indifference. 'It is ill advised, hiding your charms behind your dreams. Don't stick them there. We must not stick them there. The more we are guided in our everyday activities by life's natural forces, the more difficult it is to take us for granted. In other words, it is just going to mean more problems, yes, indeed,' I said, putting the dot on the *i* of my discourse.

And also that she should proceed to do what she had just described, as vividly as in a book. *What can be described can happen too!* She should do it, but in life this time and here, on home ground, in this small Hungarian corner of the world, and in person!

The brave little woman slid off the sofa, a decision past recall, and with the bright lights of Angel's Ground, the working-class district from whence she hailed, sparkling in her merry eyes, she gazed deep into mine. Then just as she was about to reach the door she spun round. 'Well?' I asked. 'The world is the totality of facts, not of things,' she said. Her face was inscrutable. I listened well into the night. (The walls have ears – mine).

I do hate myself a *bit* because on occasion I do a good deed from sheer vanity. Women are quite able to make friends with a man;

but to preserve such a friendship – that no doubt requires the assistance of a slight physical antipathy. I must be getting old and *ugh*ly, as the Lithuanian says.

If you have done any reading, have travelled, or to go one step further, have *lived*, then you know what a small town is like, the *Hotel* with the sonorous name, and you know how time passes there of an evening, and the night too as you wait for the merciful deliverance of morning, unwelcome as it may be. But man is an ungrateful creature and if in the morning he gets only what's coming to him for his fifty-forint victuals, and even that stale or soggy, he grumbles and for a second feels *fully* European as he pitches into the outrageously negligent staff. (Which reminds me: May Europe go to the devil, and then, *by definition*, up to the Urals!)

The hotel where I was quartered in the course of my umpteenth misguided attempt to educate the masses (to *enlighten* them!) went by the name of The Red Star, and said Red Star lived up to its name.

The woman I'm about to make the subject of my story was the hotel's chief attraction. When her embonpoint bounced playfully across the linoleum-tile floor of the restaurant all heads turned, like so many sunflowers. During the day she'd lounge on the shore of the thermal lake in a fire-engine-red bikini, casting meaningful glances (with every glanceful worth its weight in gold) at the trade union miners, who were staying there gratis in the hopes of gaining relief in the medicinal waters for whatever ailed them. A glance or two, and the tray began to tremble in the local waiter's hands as he carried glasses filled to the brim with Calvados. The miners told many a merry tale about the woman, about how she'd never spend the night alone, and that she was a match for any man because (so the miners said) it took a real man to please her, this being her *guiding principle*.

In the bar, a cross between a farmer's co-op and a mid-century brothel, she soon singled me out and to me this was like a duel. The eyes of all the miners gleamed like so many black diamonds. She looked vaguely familiar, and when, overeager, she slid her hand under the table, I suddenly knew why. Many years before, in her capacity as a nurse, she had looked after my mother, but she seemed aloof then, callous, indifferent. My younger brother and I called her Sweet Charity, an overstatement if ever there was one.

'Well, well, why this change'? I asked with a touch too much vexation, perhaps, my nose into my glass of bitters, 'why this transformation from a kind-hearted, independent young lady into a man-eating *femme fatale*, well?'

'When in my nineteenth year, barely two months in a virginally fresh marriage, my hubby cheated on me in the most despicable manner and didn't just heap lie upon lie either, cheating on me and taking all I had, he *betrayed me, betrayed me, betrayed me* . . . Anyway, my husband a manchild himself, got the boot, though he whined like a dog, and I decided to live as free as you men, independent come hell or high water, but without making too much of it either, taking all of life's gifts, the good things along with the bad jokes, rolling with the punches, as something I deserve. I am a lady, the heroine of my own life. Such was my decision.

'The world and life are one. I am my world.

'I had to tell you this by way of introduction.

'In a country like this, where I can't afford to do as I please, to say the least, I am better off, and I don't mean to *bitch*, if I live, work and study in the socialist manner. *Everyone here, myself included, is so frightfully normal.* But when summer comes,' and here my old acquaintance heaved such a snort of a sigh from behind her two hooters I held my peace with something like awe, 'I go in search of a man, a man I *want*. I have my fling, with no room for tearful farewells. After all, we make no promises, but those' – and she guffawed, though this was obviously not the first time she had said it, 'we keep, ha! ha! . . .

'Now, too, on my way down from [*self-censored*], a tunnel literally sucked me in. Anybody who's been sucked in like that knows no matter how prepared you are it is *elementally unexpected.*' I try to compensate for the terror in my body with a momentary stretch, more insolent than playful.

'But only for a moment! Because just then I feel two hot hands groping between my thighs. I'm too experienced to have *that* frighten me, though it does. Face to face, the officer (*Platzkarte!*) had to mount me on his knees, of course. He kissed the hem of my skirt, a regular Parsifal. It turned bright again just as rudely as it had turned dark before. Of his confusion the officer gave no sign. A hero from head to toe, and I went all giggly. He looked at my teeny-weeny silver panties gleaming in the dark recesses of my crotch as one bewitched. SILVER IS MY COLOUR!!! Then without betraying the least sign of embarrassment, as if offering me a cigarette, he began to flick the lips of my whatnot. He soon found what his trembling fingers sought.

'Since anyone might have caught us at it, whether a civilian or a member of the corps, an officer or a common private, and the situation too was escalating, so to speak, I rejected the initial impulse to teach the impudent rascal a lesson he wouldn't soon forget. *There are things one can and cannot do!* So as a kind of revenge I began to take my pleasure in the prodding of his finger.

'I raised my fanny to facilitate the search, but then suddenly it all seemed so *lacking*, impersonal, incorporeal and contrived, I wanted to scream and fall on that damned phallocrat with my ten fingernails. *Lacking, lacking, lacking!* On the run, I dragged him to the car's lavatory. The space was so tiny, filthy and drab, it was hardly *dignified* for two, especially when there's more on their minds than washing their anguished little hands in the manner of ill-tempered Pilates.

'The officer, his manhood [*self-censored*] under his funny-looking cotton undies, was of our fathers' generation. The decorations on his chest jingled every time he [*self-censored*].

'At the station they were waiting for both of us. We got off, one after the other, just like strangers. I liked that. Before he reached those waiting for him, I whispered wickedly, "for if there is nothing to distinguish a thing, I cannot distinguish it either, since otherwise it would be distinguished after all . . ." ' As he turned around I could see how scared he was, which made me want him so bad, I felt a hot spasm in my gut. But by then I had regained my sense of humour. So there!

'This frivolous and imprudent eagerness of mine to rush head-long into affairs of this kind is not easy, though. It is difficult. Not like the bright light of the sun at all, but like abject poverty. Most of all, it is like a child's desperate clinging to the person nearest him because he is scared of being abandoned . . . *I feel uprooted because I am the root.* There is a certain tension swelling inside me that only another can drain off, like the blood-conduit on a sword. And in such cases I don't ask who you are, where you come from, or what sort you are. You are so you may be!' Then she gazed solemnly at me saying, 'MAKE ME, MAKE ME FREE!'

I gazed at her face, by now slightly bloated, her cute little turned-up nose and generously applied eye make-up, and gave a helpless shrug. She had no hold over me. I was nearing the end of my bitters as the time, corrupt and decayed, passed at a snail's pace. She was still talking.

'I visit Kenya once a year, where an enchanting brown-skinned man waits to do my bidding. Who has not toyed with the idea of letting himself go in earnest once, at least once in his life, throwing caution to the wind, which is in his interest, and beat the flaccid privates of his life in the face of this whole damn rigmarole! Slam it all down, gloves, brigade records, the daily papers with their frigging (you should excuse me) prevarications, to delight in a new beginning *someplace else*, among the palms, in a salt-sea daze! To leave all this behind, where you can neither live nor die, as the great poet has so rightly said – no, no, no! – where, to give just one current example, you can't even get a decent blood pudding any more and the cocky waiter looks at you as if you were off your rocker. And they lie, too, needless to say.

'For instance, I have this friend. She's at the HÓDIKÖT. She travels the world with the same purpose in mind. At first it was just a dream, but then she told the foreman to go you know where and packed and left for Spain that same day. (She happened to have a window in her passport that opened on to the world. Lucky, or what?!) Though she left her broken heart behind because she still felt a secret passion for the foreman. Besides, everything had gone wrong. Her parents didn't understand her, and she felt that even in the KISZ her young communist comrades, *kissing* pals, were passing the proverbial ball back and forth so they could hit it back and congratulate themselves on their achievement. It was more than she could take, though she had what you might call a regular life, a bed-sitter, a job. And she didn't stick out from the collective either. These things were behind her, and ahead . . . What is ahead for us? The sun, the sea, the sand, the waves, as lovely as the Crimean Peninsula or the Yukon Peninsula. We went with the brigade after they gave us the Golden Wreath for Outstanding Labour for the third time. And we didn't even cheat!'

'People there work to live, and not the other way around, like here.'

'You mean we live to work? Is that what you're trying to say?'

We work to work, but I did not wish to *pursue* the *point* just yet.

'So what is the Kenyan or Iberian male like?' I ventured.

'For one thing, indubitably southern. And a hunter. Instinctive. Got the knack. And goes for it more, too, though not *necessarily* better. Passion is often simply an innate lack of discipline.'

'Anyway, you've come back, and now you're here. What is your life like? How do you two get on?'

'With difficulty.'

Sweet Charity stood up. My glass of bitters was depleted. 'The tacit conventions on which the understanding of everyday language depends are enormously complicated,' she announced, calling over her alabaster shoulder.

The next morning I took the staff to task. There they stood shifting from one foot to the other while I prodded my obligatory sunny-side-up with my fork.

Some people are such awful grouches, really, regarding everything from their own petty point of view, selfishly amplifying the shady side of progress and of life; they forget to think how the glorious new problems engendered by the new solutions could be solved in new ways; they forget that their problems today are problems *worthy* of them, from which it follows that their dissatisfaction should be society-worthy too. Instead, impatient, they'd rather lash at their horses with a whip, whereupon no one would be as surprised as they themselves to see the self-same horses, chock-full of *horse*-power, take off like the very devil . . .

Life's got to be lived, no two ways about it. Ethics and theory are not to be confused. If good or bad intentions can change the world, they can only change its boundaries, and not the facts. Not the things that can be expressed through language. Which means that the world must *generally* become something entirely different. It must condense or grow as an *entirety*. The world of happiness is not the same as the world of unhappiness. Happiness must be squeezed out of life, and no excuse.

It chanced that I became a steward, upon rather favourable conditions, I might add, on a small boat that around here is referred to as a luxury liner, which luxury liner rode the waves of the Danube and the Balaton as its mood dictated, with my compatriots looking for a little rest and relaxation aboard. *Hungarians.*

'Away with the tow-ropes!' the captain thundered, which I cheerfully interpreted in my own way . . . So then, I am here, I'm okay, I go for myself in a *really big* way. My body ditto. Those who know me know I'm no Mr Universe. But I can take a bit of strain. I am rocking and swaying atop the back of the water now, mixing drinks, because that's how life has its fling – with me and with itself.

'*Steward, six gin and tonics on the sun deck!*' burps the loudspeaker. Work ahoy! I fling down my pen, mix the drinks pronto, slam them on a tray, and there I go, prose in motion, scooting past, up up and away. And then the tray just about comes tumbling out of my hands like the leaves off a tree in autumn seeing how, next to the three young men who had previously made a special point of imprinting my image in their mind's eye, three first-class minxes are lounging butt-naked on the deck chairs. Life's beneficiaries, I should think.

As I go about my business I note every little detail down to the last hair. I look. I see. Luscious little bed-bunnies stewing in the sun. It's not *me* that's going to be squeezed dry today, I think with discipline. Everything perfect, relatively speaking, unless, of course, for that touch of the *grand mal* on the faces!

And then, as I lean over a table, I feel one of the lotus blossoms slip a piece of paper into a my paper-sensitive hands as a meaningful glance flashing from the velvety almond eyes hits the mark, eyes in which I detect a touch of sadness. A rift in Time.

But it is no easy matter reading the missive. The boys on deck are drinking faster than I can mix. They keep me on my toes. It is late afternoon (Petőfi Radio is about to launch into *Fifth Gear! Youth – Culture – Politics*) by the time the unfolding can proceed behind the mahogany counter. *The note was written in stilted language, in a trembling hand (pro domo*: as indeed, this whole chapter)! 'Dear Sir/Comrade/Man! Must help! We are not what we seem. Not easy, but other. The men, S.O.B.s from ÁFÉSZ general co-op on shore with open and/or unopen persuasion ambushed us out of clothes, LIKE WALNUT FROM PEEL, with excuse they will raise our pay raises. Which alas is true, so we are in their hands. We will not be ungrateful!'

Well, I'll be dingled!! What a fix! and I simply had to help the three graces; what I mean is, I had to help them *simply* . . . Yes, but *how?*

I mixed the three turkey cocks a democratic 'snooze cocktail' on the sly. It would have floored a horse. They imbibed the devilish brew . . . All I had to do now was find the captain's antidote, who was standing guard on deck, to cover the villainy. Carefully, pretending friendship, I knocked on his shoulder, then, as he turned around, a little less friendly, on his chin. Over the rail and into the water. Hope to Neptune he can swim!

Now there was nothing left but the squeezing. When we were by ourselves (the girl had wisely seen to that) she with the almond eyes fell at my feet. 'My hero! I am yours!' So that's where we stand. What could the answer be, I wondered. And was what we *generally* call an answer possible at all? 'Look,' I said, 'a piece of me leaves so it can be with you, provided you accept me as someone who is With You.' She nodded gently. She wetted her lips. And suddenly this nothing of a female became all important to me. I would have hated her, had she not loved me. *Hurry! Hurry! Just let's not rush into it!*

'Dialogue, my child, is possible only if the partners step out of anonymity and *bring about* a combat-worthy ground upon which, lying on the *horizontal* of the personal, neither on this nor the other side of it, neither in the sphere of the abstract nor in the non-personal, allows what can be said inside each other to become real . . . I have no false illusions in this respect, I admit it; I have to, because reality can be constraining, advancing on you like an army laying siege to a city, or like bees zeroing in on a honeycomb. In short, I say that under the given circumstances, the *tongue* could become an indispensable medium of communication, what's more, spurred on by rather mean and nasty directorial instructions. One's tongue, one's language (!) is a giant graveyard of attitudes packed chock-full of metaphor-gravestones. That's how it is. Still, the reality materialising with its help, seeing how it arches from one person to the other, speaks to a person *personally* (oh, you sweet little cuddly-pooh!). It must refer to something shared. In short, there is scope for understanding. In theory, at least.

'Come,' the young lady hissed.

Looking for the truth is always an adventure, more exhilarating than Casanova's, more exalted than Parsifal's – even better than

Timur and his band of Young Pioneers in the perennial Soviet favourite. What's gotta be worked on here is *being* together with people, *living* with them, if you know what I mean, here in Hungary;[4] so that all the riches and beauty each of us carries within like a mortal illness or a millstone around his neck we can offer others on a tray, as it were. That's why I think nothing of groups that turn inwards upon themselves, where the same thing is thrown into the light of common consciousness over and over again accompanied by a certain sense of bourgeois or proletarian self-satisfaction, drenched with the bittersweet sauce of public grievances.

'My ass is cooling off. Let's go!'

Her body pleasantly rubbing against mine, in her I soon forgot my previous anxiety. When we parted, the young lady placed her pretty little finger on her dewy lips and with a hint at the happy parents who were about to pick her up she said, 'What we cannot speak about we must pass over in silence. When virtue has slept it will arise more vigorous.'

I was drained, drained, drained, brain and groins both. It is no good being so smug and egotistical, wanting to have it all all at the same time but, to resort to a bit of imagery, to pull at the corner of the table-cloth, whereupon no one's going to be as surprised as we when the whole rigmarole comes tumbling to the ground and the sight of a piece of discarded, buttered bread being gradually soaked in the remains of some lukewarm tea comes leaping to the eye . . .

---

[4] Teacher at a parent-teacher meeting: 'This year's objective has been the moral education of our children. This objective has been successfully implemented.'

I am a man of experience. I share my experience with others. But this does not make me feel superior in any way. You have your job, I have mine. People around here are vigilant. Hungry for knowledge. What must be done comes leaping to the eye.

I'd never seen boobs so huge before, though you mustn't think of tits like a cow's or those unseemly but substantial outgrowths that should be called paired humps, rather; each of these was a real live boosiasm to boost your enthusiasm, the size only *incidental*, the way we say of a story that incidentally, it might have actually happened.

'My husband relegates me to the background,' the owner of the boobs said to me without mincing her words. I can be as surprised as the next man; this too is part of my profession. This bewitching feline creature with skin so white it reminded me of expensive Meissen porcelain ('Made in the GDR') who seemed to have stepped out of an X-rated story book for readers over 18 years of age, this *luscious hunk of flesh* could she be hungry in that certain sense?

'What does you husband do?' I asked conservatively. She heaved a great sigh and pointed to the colonial-style bookshelves. Now it was my turn to take a seat on her leatherette. 'What a question! He reads!' Whereupon I locked the fatigue-ridden colleague into my heart. 'From Péter Veres[5] to Wittgenstein he devours every-

[5] 'The most important representative of the poor peasantry among the peasant writers [who] expounded the inevitability of the coming of socialism. During the first half of his career his works concentrated on sociographic and autobiographical descriptions of the abject lives of the peasantry and the agrarian proletariat' (*cf.*, *A Concise History of Hungarian Literature*). Also Defence Minister, and from 1954 to 1956, President of the Writers Union, but let it lie . . . Wittgenstein is not mentioned in *A Concise History of Hungarian Literature*.

thing, while I sit by his side without hope, with nothing to hope for.' 'Reading you to shreds,' I added wittily. 'He does not take me seriously, that's the problem,' she said liberally. 'Fine. In that case, come along with me.'

Their nuptial chamber bore a distinct resemblance to the National Library, the only difference being that here the Yugoslav-Hungarian *New Symposion*, too liberal by half, was out on the open shelves. I gave the bookworm credit for that. 'Tell me honestly. How am I supposed to be domestically happy here?' That was the question. The situation was grave but not past praying for.

'You must snare him with his own hobby,' I said, pointing to the obvious solution. 'A book is a powerful thing,' I continued presumptuously. 'With the right books I can get the most phlegmatic couple or other formation of individuals to sit up and take note! You'll see. A book, soft lighting, Calvados, and your neglectful husband will be like a bitch in heat over love and liberty. Social responsibility *plus* petting. But take care,' and here I inadvertently made a threatening gesture, 'a book can be dangerous. If you light his fire, you'd better have enough fire-wood!' Sure of herself now, the woman laughed. 'Or other combustible material.' I said nothing. Why think of the worst right away? After all, there are more things in heaven and earth Horatio, and all that jazz.

Suddenly I felt an irresistible urge to read something out loud from the Nyugat's third generation. I just couldn't help myself. 'World literature. And *unadulterated*,' I said succinctly and seriously. I opened one of the books I knew practically by heart to a specific place, allowing the author to come to his words. His paeans to beauty were anything but prudish; instead of fiddling around, he called things by their names. *Life*, he said. *Love*, he said. *Liberty*, he said. And they *exist*, he said. But he did so with such a disarming lack of artifice, no one could possibly take offence. The woman listened willingly. 'Don't squirm,' I said. The severity was pretended.

'It is to be hoped that you are speaking the truth,' blondie said. 'I hanker after it *so*.'

'I don't wonder. But should your husband not respond to these, may I suggest a handsomely illustrated picture book from the impressive prose crop of the sixties? In these are pictured for the *general* edification, colossal and mammoth things of beauty along with truths that'll abso–fuckin'–lutely ball him over, if you'll excuse the expression. Like a fine champagne does it work on the male. And mind you. I am not thinking of anything unseemly, but of the incandescent aesthetic of life seen in the raw.' She kept her silence. Because I am proud, I was determined to break it. 'How about a touch of privatization from the pseudo–romantic pseudo-prosperity of the seventies, degraded into *domestic* politics?' I suggested shrewdly. 'That's where the dog lies buried!'

'Dog?!' snickered the frustrated lady. 'Horse. You mean horse, not dog.' That got me thinking. That instead of *barking* we should be *pulling*. Is that what she was trying to tell me? But at the time she was not yet talking.

There soon came another time, though, when she was as perky as a glass of bubbly, her gait was as light as a feather, her shiny hair aglow with a thousand fairy lights, while her laughter was wild and forceful. (Daring, attractive, desperate.)

'You are a magician!' she shouted at me, and to be perfectly honest, it felt good hearing it. Not that I've got anything to complain about, mind you. My writings get published, the reviews are generally kind, and if they're not, I can always think of it as a good sign, see, I am worth writing about. Some women are so very deeply *stormy*, I thought very deep down.

'*Du musst dein Leben ändern*,' I shouted along with Rilke. You must change your life.

'It's happened, it's happened,' she screeched, her small feline face turning purple. 'Yes,' I said softly. The rest we can leave to the imagination. Then the little lady turned on her heels.

'*The riddle* does not exist.'

'That's what *you* think,' said I in my heart of hearts.

A friend of mine, a Party member who had a certain reputation because though he had been repeatedly forced to step aside during the stormy ebb and tide of the Working Class Movement – furthermore, *why cover it up*, for lack of experience he had even been *tragically in error* himself; suffice it to say, in him the fire of faith rages undiminished, the yearning to serve, and a fervent hope, too, for the future; he is a functionary who lives *with* the people, being one of them, except that his feeling of responsibility is greater, of course, it being a function of his high position; and he knows, too, that he is no sugar-daddy, no Uncle Sam flinging handouts of chocolate bunnies to his people, oh, no! he turns to them *with requests*, a guide, a shepherd with clear purpose in mind, calling upon them to work for their common and mutual benefit, and in him the pain that comes from the conviction that here and now some immense and formidable historical prospect is at stake is genuine, too. In short, he is a true communist, and the following story comes from him. I quote.

'When the attractive, young and impetuous brunette, a working girl from the workers' district with the sonorous name <an angel from Angel's Ground> came to see me during my office hours, she glanced at me with suspicion forthwith. "I must tell you honestly forthwith," she said honestly forthwith, "I have no great confidence in politicians." "Oh," I said taken aback, because I was not used – no, not to the straight talk, but there was a strange determination in her voice, pain and hatred combined, which was addressed to me as well, and this was not a pleasant feeling, and that's what I was not used to. "You have such a deep aversion to politicians?"

' "To all who see in me nothing but a political object, a guinea pig of social advancement, regardless of whom we are talking about. Well, we are talking about me! me! me! Why is it so hard to understand? A person can have good friendly relations without immediately thinking of *class*. A mother is not a countess or a peasant! But all the politicians I have had the ill fortune to meet were not satisfied, treating me or the situation as a sovereign entity; right away they think of the p . . . and other revolting abstractions. They got one-track minds. Besides, it's *me* that wants freedom, me, me me! and not the kind neither that's broken down into centrally planned, quarterly production quotas or is dependent upon the dubious loopholes of your petty, shabby world of small, glittering private business enterprises. Goulash capitalism indeed! Comrade, they say to me, don't be impatient, *your freedom quotient is satisfactory*. Compared to the average, in fact . . . Well, it is *not* satisfactory, see?!" (The dignity of the spirit owes it to itself to scorn any power that would limit its actions, I said behind the lock and key of my heart.)

' "Oh-oh, it's not going to be an easy day, young lady. Are you trying to tell me that everything concerning the p . . . is revolting?"

' "Precisely. As far as I'm concerned, at any rate. What others think is no business of mine."

' "And oppression?"

' "I knew you'd bring that up. I could've sworn. Why don't you go throw in the advanced state of democracy for good measure, and *floor* me. But don't you be thinking I'm hypocritical, giving unconditional preference to our p . . . provided, of course . . ."

' "Provisions? You come with provisions?!"

"That's just it! Your way of thinking lacks the drive towards wholeness. And I find that revolting. I have no wish to be the ruling class. Be good enough and remember that."

'Oh, no, you mustn't my little cuddly-pooh . . . As might be expected, after a while I posed the question, is she looking for *social* satisfaction at all . . . Because, or so I argued, lots of people do it, or let others do it to them, out of self-interest, friendship, because they're rats, out of compassion, or the devil knows . . .

' "No. I don't do it and won't let others do it to me. For me it's not a red herring, for me it's a nightmare. I want to steer clear of such murky waters."

' "I see. Neither one way nor another. But if you don't mind my saying so, you're much too naïve. Surely, little girl, you're no vestal virgin yourself . . . But then, there *is* another way out, is there not?"

' "That's my own affair. And none of your damned business."

' "Have you ever had anything to do with [*self-censored*]?"

' "I seem to recall something. But the memory of it is filled only with pain, and not a trace of pleasure."

' "And afterwards?"

' "You can imagine very well for yourself, *documentary*-like, after what happened, I was in no mood to go back for seconds."

' "Naturally, such vehement transformations can be accompanied by pain. Though not invariably. Sometimes the conviviality outweighs the pain, sometimes the other way around. And sometimes they're equal, and sometimes there's no knowing."

' "Well, it's painful. So why do it like *that* again?"

' "Why? To sound and probe the bottom of it and see whether the triple watchword of *l'amour* and *liberté* might not light your fire. Of course, I do not mean to lecture you. If you're happy like this . . ."

' *"Happy? What's happy?"*

'Oh, more often than I could count does the picture come popping into my mind as the little steely-eyed butt-peddler says to me, turning on her heels, "The object is simple." Then she gives her scrawny little shoulders a conclusive shrug.'

My friend finished his story. For a long time we said nothing. We drank red wine. At last, I spoke.

'When the answer cannot be put into words, neither can the question be put into words. *The riddle* does not exist. If a question can be framed at all, it is also *possible* to answer it . . . Scepticism is not *irrefutable*, but obviously nonsensical, when it tries to raise doubts where no question can be asked. For doubt can exist only where a question exists, a question only where an answer exists, and an answer only where something can be *said*.'

My friend did not see eye to eye with me. Meanwhile, it had gradually grown dark, as if it were dawning backwards, then, like a dense veil falling from the starry sky, silence returned. Politely but emphatically, I threw him out. I needed to work, because when I am working, my heart overflows with the milk of human kindness.

II
(anecdote)

> *Do not lift the veil of your illusions.*
> *Stay innocent, a blissful dreamer,*
> *for a dream that stays a dream is still*
> *a whole lot better than a future that*
> *cannot be dreamt at all.*
> *Hugs and kisses,*
> *Mom and Kuki*

Preface
(to be read with anger)

Though our profession is august, there is ample scope for the observation of humorous events that unwittingly offer themselves up for scrutiny. In the following stories sacred truth and colourful poetry dovetail, and so ample spiritual benefit, pious instruction and pleasurable artistic experience are *a priori* guaranteed, despite the author's shortcomings.[6]

[6] We wish to mention here that Charles IX was so expert at minting counterfeit coins that in this respect he even dumbfounded the connoisseur. 'It is our great good luck,' said the Archbishop of Lotharingia, 'that out of the goodness of his heart he has seen fit to show *himself* some mercy.'

I have gone over the top, I think. On the other hand, the top had it coming. But in order to write this section, I was in need of an inordinate amount of profound, celestial gaiety, because I can scale the highest peaks of pathos only if it is a *game*. (In the end *there is light at the end of the tunnel*.)

The word *anecdote* is Greek in origin. It means 'unpublished'. Being unpublished does not mean that these stories have never been published or are not going to be published, just that they had been *left out*, relegated to oblivion, because they are not sufficiently *official* and do not aspire to the standards of some dignified, bearded authority.

In short, an anecdote is a historical joke. The ones here are, concretely, Hungarian.

Still, whether we read them in one stretch, like a novel, or dip into them from time to time, certain recurrent melodies, centuries-old melodies ring out. First and foremost the longing for and love of liberty, the disdain and parody of injustice, the respect due to courage mixed with just a touch of brazenness, composure in grave distress and flaring passions in the small, and as the shared tonality in all these melodies, beside the *major* chord of battles and political skirmishes, the *minor* chord of humour. Irony. Irony, as Musil says, is when we describe a cleric so that the Bolshevik becomes our target as well, or if a half-wit, so that the author should also feel, well if that isn't partly me! This type of irony – constructive irony – is relatively unknown in today's Hungary. This naked irony emerges from the relationship of things. Irony is generally regarded as sarcastic and derisive. The joke I welcome most is that which stands in place of a weighty not altogether harmless thought, at once a cautionary gesture of the finger and a flashing of the eye.

If I can provide my readers with a few pleasurable hours, I shall be genuinely gratified. But above all, I am driven by an inner compulsion to leave nothing unsaid that might bear with the least significance, especially for those who are fighting for a freer human existence. The truth shall remain the truth even if coloured by my feelings and value judgements. *Possibly what for me is a labyrinth is, for others, a good prospect!*

To remember is a formidable obligation. Once I am gone in wake of the others what I have forgotten or neglected to write down will disappear without a trace. As Rabelais says, *Depuis n'en fut parlé. La mémoire en expira avec le son des cloches lesquelles quadrillonuerent à son enterrement.* (No one spoke of him after that. His memory expired with the sound of the bells ringing at his funeral.) . . . You might call this a memoir. A medley of memories. A flotsam and jetsam medley of memoir fragments. And then, by definition, *my* flaunt-some-get-some medley of memoir fragments. In which case, of course, I should begin accordingly, the way Witold Gombrowicz begins his notes: *I.I.I.I.* – But never mind. Let us look instead at the blood-splattered facts of life that around these parts are so much in evidence, having become our daily bread, our common fare.

Take note, though! I published nothing at the time. From '49 on not a single line appeared from my pen, and I can prove it! Of course, I did not do any writing either, though I am not sure whether this will sufficiently excuse the narrow-sightedness of our former cultural policy. The direct relationship between word and deed was severed, as Béla Hamvas writes in another place,

in a work which to this day has remained in manuscript form –
and cuts our lives in twain. *The determination that must compel
each and every one of our decisions has yet to be learned.*

And so I kept mum, though truth to tell, not from malice, not
even from squeamishness; I wouldn't want to give all this some
sort of moral *bouquet* after the fact as a number of my esteemed
colleagues have done. My pen simply did not take to paper. I
realise this sounds romantic (because it's like I'm saying God
was watching over me) but the truth is, *quasi*, that I simply didn't
know *how* to write. My friend Simon Barbocz's comment comes
to mind, the one he dropped before our attempt to switch sides
in '44: 'We can't write all our impotence off to the German
presence in Hungary.' (He was a young man with burning eyes
and a long scarf around his neck who generally saved his wise
pronouncements for the dawn's early light . . . Oh, the strange
ecstasy of dawn! Well into his cups, Simon shouted how the
Germans this and the Germans that; they could have taken him
away at any time, nor did he really say 'our impotence', he said,
'this impotent cock-sucking'.)

But getting back to the fifties, Minister of Culture Révai, who
was a mightily gifted and worthy man but who – and this must
be added for the sake of accuracy – also caused horrendous
damage *objectively speaking* (the source of his tragedy, the Révai
tragedy!) mercilessly nipped my first attempt to scale the heights
of literature in the bud. OTTO TOTTERED, TONTO TIT-
TERED, I wrote practically at the start of my career, and he,
meaning Révai, saw in this a *tendency* towards Habsburg resto-
ration – need I say how unjustly? not to mention the fact there
is no *knowing, really*, who tottered and who tittered, am I right,
or am I right?

We met in person just once, God only knows with how many guileful and underhanded detours. Gyula[7] was the first to be appraised, then he told the neighbourhood greengrocer, who, as he was cheating me out of six forints and seventy fillérs in change, happened to mention it to me. At first this subtle chain of disclosures eluded me, but after a while I finally got the message (and put the blame where blame belonged), and so on . . . 'A typical young man today would die laughing. But be careful, my young friend! If you don't want your laughter to fall back on your head, like when you spit in the wind then stand under it, your laughter must be highly differentiated. *Historically*, I might add. Besides, as you shall see, you won't be able to articulate too many opinions to your liking. The study of vulgar times results in a lean catharsis . . . Of course, what does vulgar mean anyhow?'

I waited a long time in the huge reception room, but it was so obvious they were keeping me waiting on purpose, it made me laugh. (Alas, too soon!) Révai is an educated man of the world, I reflected, surely he knows what Nietzsche had to say on the subject. A sure means of irritating people and putting evil thoughts into their heads is to keep them waiting a long time. To have this happen makes one immoral. My patience was the conceit of a man of the spirit who thinks he can see through the machinations of power, what I mean is, those machinations that in his pride he calls by that name. And true enough, he does see right through them. Except in the meantime the *other* sees right through *him* as well. Each sees right through the other.

[7] Last name Illyés (1901–1983), author of *The People of the Puszta*. Considered a classical writer in his lifetime, and a sort of father-figure. I considered him one myself.

Which calls for a certain amount of circumspection . . . Of course, I would not go so far as to call this mutual deceit *the dual triumph* of realism. For one thing, Rajk[8] was still alive at the time.

Anyway, it never occurred to me that I was about to *buckle under*. Thanks to my newly acquired self-confidence I had just decided that there was no need to sprawl stentoriously in the armchair, leaning back and stretching my legs out with adolescent abandon. Instead, I sat in relative safety, 'uptight', knees pressed together. (To this day I can hear a screeching female voice from the past, my mother's or my Czech aunt's; I never understood what could be so unsettling in the way one *sits*, it must have been some form of compensation for male slovenliness, not to mention the indubitable fact that the upholstery did get *hideously* rumpled.)

Yet buckle under I did, though I was not that impressed – not with myself, at any rate. The strength of my own youthful years, the giddiness of the New Beginning, the historical imperative of the remorseless dispensation of Justice, these did not awe me, the heroic acts that were shaping the nation, et cetera. There is a real sense of freedom in flinging it in their faces, mercilessly, telling these people how our kind feels living among them . . . *I will have no part in this*, I would have liked to say, and in such a way that it should also prove to be a *solution* of sorts, at least for me.

But that's not how it was. Because I am intimidated. Fine. But

[8] First name László (1909–1949), member of the Hungarian Communist Party, secretary of the Central Committee of the Party after 1944, Minister of Domestic Affairs, then Minister of Foreign Affairs. In May of 1949 he was arrested on trumped-up charges and was sentenced to death as a provocateur. (*Cf. The Denunciation.*) The rest is history. But it was quite a 'show' while it lasted.

it happens to be *me* that's intimidated, not just anybody I can look down my nose at or feel sorry for just like that, out of the goodness of my heart. *What's to become of me? That is the question.* Because I remember walking down Andrássy Road, past number 60 once, anxious in the shadow of the infamous ÁVÓ head-quarters, yet trying to be stoical, yet quickening my steps when, as it was about to leave, I caught a glimpse of myself in the window of a big black *furtive* automobile *scooting past, there goes prose scooting past!* said I in my heart promptly and courageously, and also, *prose scared stiff of a punch on the nose*; now as I write it, I am muttering to myself once again, prose on the nose, and feel the former movement of my lips . . . And then, abruptly, as I looked at the sidewalk, it hit me how somebody must have hurried past here just a while ago, somebody *on his way to work*, to number 60; I rubbed the soles of my feet against the asphalt, and the thought that the traces of our steps were *mingling* like that gave way to a nasty sort of fear, and then, further, that the air, that we're breathing the same air, that maybe what he was *ex*haling just then I was *in*haling, or the other way around. Appalling! Over the top, that's what this sort of fraternising is. Because there are murderers, and there are victims. But hold! Conscience doth make wiseguys of us all. You're either a writer, or. . . . We're a nation of horsemen. We know how to stroke a bull by the horn.

In my show of confidence I even grinned at one of the shamuses, but he did not react quite as I had expected; he looked back at me pointedly, even taking a step towards me like a hoodlum, but then he backed away with such insouciance, I might have thought it was accidental. And so I did not know what to think at all. I sat in the damp leatherette armchair, from time to time losing my balance, and when the large, white French door swung open I expected to see an elegant, gaunt secretary wearing a skinny tie and an ulcerous expression (the highly elaborate character of this fantasy is a dead give-away, a product of inhibitions that spring from fear), or else a faithful, sad-eyed secretary with glasses, a big hulk of frustrated womanhood (later gone mad, put in solitary, *a giant Soviet ovary!* she yelped the whole day long; *cf.* the piece entitled *Clitical exercise*); instead, Révai himself poked his dishevelled head through the door, running his fingers through his hair in the manner of a distraught teacher, his searching eyes hurriedly taking in the large waiting room, then coming to rest on my person, come – come – come, he waved, and with the same gesture, still from behind the door and without ever leaving the room (as if he were hiding something, or was in negligée or whatever), he gave the shamus a good dressing down, screaming, you mop-head, you yes-man, why did you keep him waiting! but this too he curtailed abruptly, without transition, '*my apologies,*' he said, contrite and impatient, 'I have a racking headache, but what would you know about that, young people don't get headaches.'

'I do,' I said, and this was like licking ass. He apologised for keeping me waiting, if anyone, he knows what it's like waiting, but he was smiling in the meanwhile as if to say, well, we're over *that* bit now. In short, or so it seemed to me, he was making me his accomplice. (What an idea, I'd now say.) Also, I felt sorry for him because of the pain, the haggard face, the dull muteness of the eyes, the familiar signs, I felt sorry for him and hated him too right away, because his whole purposeless drifting between pain and complicity, courage and betrayal, this uncontained surging tide of ambiguity suddenly looked to me very much like a *method.*

Which attained its end. Révai noticed my embarrassment and

gave an almost imperceptible frown, surely thinking what a weakling of a lad I was, and then, again just an unexpectedly, he conjured up a banana out of thin air. 'Go ahead, eat,' he said, 'it'll calm your nerves.'

A banana! In the fifties! Which just added to my confusion, of course. What would I do, I tried to remember, if I were in my right mind, if the situation were in *its* right mind, but drew a blank. After all, hardly had a few moments passed, and already so many good things had happened to me. An intelligent gentleman suffered in ways familiar to me, while I could munch voluptuously on an exotic fruit – (but) like a schoolboy that swallowed the canary! (Stalinism, I have read someplace, has made efficacious use of certain *fitting* techniques of Catholicism.)

Anyway, that's how it was. The rest is of little interest. I was picking at the inside of the banana skin while Révai pumped me. Why am I so *provisional*, why this shilly-shallying, this evasiveness, this shying away, this wariness, why this stalling and aversion, what's happened to my guts, why don't I *check* with them before I act, synchronise my intentions, why am I behaving in such a pitiful manner, and why am I so squeamish, why do I make such a fuss, why don't I *go* for it, feather my nest, what's wrong with a career, anyway, and why am I not worth even troubling about?

He used the formal form of address, which surprised me because till then (and to this day) only *mature women* are this formal with me. No first names for them! He fell silent, which meant it was my turn to speak. 'Have I given you false hope against my will? I am an arable land,' I wanted to say pathetically, but typically, suspecting a piece of Germanism, I relented. Meanwhile, my situation went from bad to worse. 'I am arable land.' Because of the subtle emphasis this, on the other hand, would have required an actor, while I wished to be nothing at all.

'I am a piece of arable land,' I said at last. But by then Révai had lost interest. 'Of course, of course . . .' I was also planning to say by way of a declaration of independence of sorts that *I will not give back the land!* but chickened out. I later heard that Révai was considerably *disaffected* with me, that he had expected more of me, but that I'm just a spoiled culture vulture of a lordling who swims with the tide, and that with the mention of that fertile piece of land, I had implicitly said as much, because the good writer casts the bad seed *from* him.

'I'm no produce wholesaler and seed classifier,' I later said to someone over a glass of beer, slightly under the influence; this got back to Révai, but by the time he could have taken revenge, the *conditions* were no longer ripe, because by then it was 1953.'

As I sit in front of my book, my grateful joy knows no bounds, for now I can hand back in one neat bundle to Hungarian society what through so many years it had itself produced. Two things, however, I wish to point out. I heard from my friend Simon Barbocz that a candidate for city council, after he'd set forth everything of merit in his policy speech, declaimed proudly and with great emphasis, 'One thing you cannot take away from me, I was also your contemporary!'

---

[9] *'Our beloved leader, he is dead, our blazing torch and lance, Stalin is dead.'* Horrific silence. (*Cf. Holiday.*) The horrific silence was partly due to the fact that many of his best pupils, including Révai, were politically 'demoted'. Rákosi held out till '56.

This goes for me, too.

That's one.

The other, honoured Reader, is that when this unfortunate Magyar nation of ours is abused and saddened (oh, those gasoline prices!) by so many or, conversely, is made to laugh or cry, it has fallen to my lot, whether with success I cannot say, to wipe off the tears, to rip the gauze from the open wounds and smooth the fevered and murderous brows hot from the sweltering sun. All good works are fathered by discontent and mothered by diligence, as they say. And it is not Goethe but Hölderlin who says: My business is to speak about the Fatherland. But this should not make me the object of envy.

There are people among us who say that whatever can be made into an anecdote is not worth the trouble; in other words, that actually, how shall I put it, the anecdote *approves* of its subject, whereas said subject, here and now, might not merit approval in the least, and anyway these things are too mysterious and disgraceful to become the object of chatter; besides, if we cannot discuss them openly, because we are the way we are and we are where we are, it is best not to discuss them at all.

There's a lot to be said for that.

And yet it might be worth our while to call attention in this manner (among others) to the bad sort of contentment so much in evidence today, thanks to our habit of taking things in stride. Some of us will surely say that this gesture of mine is just another one of these. I do not think so, though I realise how it might be misconstrued, and consider this one of its faults.

If we survey the opportunities we let slip by, our lives, we are overcome by a sense of awe. But only for a moment, and . . . and the feeling disappears, because it is to the inestimable credit of every Hungarian that he forgets the bad and likes to remember only what is good and pleasurable.

To do what we must and think as little as humanly possible about ourselves in the process – this is as much as we can do.

Dated 16th of June, Buda

Come on baby light my fire, I

Once during coalition times, after the Fulton speech (headline: 'Churchill launches verbal attack on the Soviet Union!') and in the midst of the Cold War, Mátyás Rákosi was taking a leisurely stroll through the Peace Camp when he happened to spot a couple of functionaries sitting by a great big fire. He asked them for some in order to light up. While the overcautious Social Democrats ran helter-skelter in search of a pair of tongs, a young, self-respecting *recruited worker* by the name of István Medve scooped up some embers with his bare hands and with the ashes (so he shouldn't burn his hand) he held such a beautiful burning fire up to the First Secretary, well, it was as bright as any five-pointed star! 'Now that's what I call a real man,' the first man of the realm said as he lit up from this rare sizzling pot.

Ethics

Once upon a time during the early, fun-filled fifties, Mátyás gave the imperialists such a dressing down, he later repented of it himself. And so to dispel his sadness he took a little side-trip to Munkács, not to say Mukachevo, in order to do some hunting, though not without taking a good dose of *joie de vivre* along. (I wish to mention here that Rákosi could be extraordinarily short-tempered at times. Once during a hunt, because the branch of a tree brushed against his eye, he pointed his gun at his forester. But this forester was a man of experience, and a real man to boot – for one thing, he had known Béla Kun[10] – so all he said was, 'Be kind enough, dear Comrade, sweet Comrade, to take my widow and poor orphans under your caring wings.' 'Lucky for you, impudent rascal, that you have a widow and orphans!' said the Chief Secretary generously, and placed his gun back on his shoulder.)

Anyway, at eventide, during the ride back home, one of the ÁVÓ officers in Mátyás's retinue, a tried-and-true trouper of the secret police, voiced his concern that the hunting party might have to suffer some slight delay at the Russian-Hungarian border. Meanwhile the sun set and, as it did so, these grave men quivered and shivered in the cool of the night even though just a while before they had been running helter and skelter in search of the paltriest patches of shade to seek relief from the heat.

It was turning dark practically *visibly*, and the ÁVÓ officer in question couldn't shake off the eerie feeling that the air molecules were turning dark *eye by eye*. (He had started night school but

---

[10] Kun (1886–1939): member of Russia's Bolshevik Party and in 1919 a founding member of the Hungarian Communist Party. According to *The New Hungarian Lexicon*, 'in late 1917 he went to Petersburg, then to Moscow, where he *knew* Lenin.' By 1919 he was the head of the short-lived Hungarian Republic of Councils, an offshoot of the Russian revolution. *The New Hungarian Lexicon* calls Kun 'the most important domestic representative of the Marxist-Leninist ideology of proletarian dictatorship'. No wonder.

couldn't finish. 'By nightfall all my strength was gone. Besides, the little woman was always at me about the dough.')

In the meantime, member of Mátyás's closest retinue made certain unflattering references to the activities of the green patched ÁVÓ border guards, hinting that in exchange for a smallish bribe, anyone could cross the border with ease, even if he should happen to carry objects liable to duty on him, most especially at the Russian-Hungarian frontier. Whereupon the First Secretary made public his august wish that he would very much like to be provided with *tangible proof* of what had just been said (*cf.* my *The reflection of truth: a case of overkill*).

And so it was decided that Rákosi should stay in the so-called background. (By the way, he had a veritable passion for dressing up as a secret policeman on his day off; he wore a nosegay in his cap, a satchel with bread hanging from his side, and a sword with a Hussar's pelisse flung over his shoulder. He cut a stick for himself from a cherry tree that stood by the wayside, then crossed the fields like any ordinary mortal eager to reach home and be reunited with his ageing forebears. As you can imagine, the bodyguards had more work on their hands than they knew what to do with. In this manner did Rákosi enjoy the love of his people.)

The plan was put into effect, and upon reaching the checkpoint, the ÁVÓ officer entrusted with the delicate mission jumped off the Russian buggy, and as the virginal light of the moon gleamed pristine on his gun, he fell into discourse with a young, ruddy-cheeked guard, happening to let drop that he had to cross the border in something of a rush. 'That might happen *over there*,' said the hight-spirited youth, who day after day found joy in service, loved staying up nights, and took pleasure in the troop alerts that would have tried anyone's manhood, the rough jokes, the coolish early-morning breeze and the mighty roar of the deep, dark forest while, with equal vehemence, he hated the unspecified enemies of the people – 'provided you have nothing to declare, Comrade!'

'But that's just it. 'Cause I happen to have on me a *coup'la pounds* of candles, sugar, coffee, blue jeans and some o' them cute little calculators. But I wouldn't like – how shall I put it – to waste a single minute on account of it.' But the youth stood his ground. 'What are you thinking of, my good man, my dear Comrade?! That would entail a serious breach of honour!' (How very true!)

Terrified at his prospective failure, like the silvery vapour trail of a snail did the cold sweat slither down the forehead of the secret policeman. His eyes, bulging and *fixed in place*, seemed to mesmerise the youth. (This *fixing in place* was a simple precaution on his part, as in those days it would often happen that someone would be told, 'Your eyes are shifting all over the place,' in which case you could be damned sure that the Comrade whose eyes were *supposedly [m.e.]* shifting all over the place would come under suspicion, for whoever heard of smoke where there is no fire?)

The moon shone as dispassionately as if it couldn't care less which would triumph, Truth or Falsehood, when the stalwart youth who had turned a deaf ear to the tempting promises now lay his last card on the table: 'Not for all the money in the world!' And at that time that was a lot of money, believe you me.

At this point in our story, Mátyás Rákosi, whom, despite his camouflage, the ruddy-cheeked guard recognised in a flash, sprang forth from behind the bushes. Saluting, the guard waited for further orders. '*Kharasho*, that-a-boy, boy,' shouted Mátyás gleefully, 'a vigilant columnist, if ever there was one (it was late, and he was tired), detecting the enemy like that even behind a mask!' Well, that made the ÁVÓ officer feel hot under the collar, and wouldn't you know, the very next day he disappeared without a trace.

Rákosi expanded his chest. The beasts of the wild and the birds of the air desisted with their natural noises. 'Comrades! There are many things, too, too many things, that are far from clear in this and similar instances!' The lad shuffled his feet in his oversize boots, one hand on the butt of his gun, the other on the seam of his pants; preoccupied, the First Secretary crumbled a dried twig between his stubby fingers as he laughed good-heartedly at the guard's embarrassment.

'Well, fella, am I your fella?' The autumn woods stirred briefly to life. 'Your chest is wide enough, dear Comrade, plenty of room for a medal or two.' And with that he motioned to his retinue, and the comrades took their beautiful dolmans off, and there were as many sparkling precious stones on those dolmans as poppy seeds on a bun.

Soon, alas too soon, did the illustrious company disappear through the clear geometric grid of searchlights that pierced the body of the thick dark forest, intricately lovely, reminiscent of a Moholy-Nagy. But Rákosi turned back to the fatigued lad one last time. 'In today's Hungary,' he intoned, 'real spring is in the air!'

As our man stood dumbfounded, his heart racing in the dark, a hard night descended upon him. In a sky chiselled smooth by the wind, like a pane of Formica, the stars showed like silver flakes, tarnished now and again by the yellow gleam of a revolving light. Perfumes of spice and warm stone were wafted on the breeze. Then, like a dense veil slowly falling from the starry sky, silence returned, and he was free to do at last what the illustrious personage had advised: to go through life with a song in his heart.

Just a kiss, do gimme a kiss

What happened, and why? these are the twin questions that concern expert and humble populace alike, and rightly too if we are to learn about our past, thereby giving ourselves a chance for the present. Admittedly, there is much to be done in this respect. Luckily, I happen to have in my hands an important document concerning the genesis in question.

It happened soon after what we call the Liberation . . . Before the Russian army moved in, we had known life only from photographs, as it were, which, as we know, have no smell and do not make a filthy mess. But then we fell into that big, lukewarm, muddy, malodorous–putrid swamp called Life.

Life came to greet us in the shape of women, drink, good times and good company, and we did our best to oblige. We thronged the pubs, the theatres, the concert halls, attended genteel teas, blue-collar gigs, society balls and servants' dance halls, the famous Buzelka, the ill-reputed Bean Soup Csárda, and in a concerted effort to add polish to our ideological sophistication, at dawn's early light we read (because we had to), at the factories and offices (because we had to), in enthusiastic unison (because we had to) the Party daily *Szabad Nép*. (With pathos, to the lecturer: Instead of raising your voice, Comrade, if you'd just make sure all this actually got into the *Szabad Nép*, Comrade, the *Free People*, Comrade, it would be a whole lot better for us, Comrade, and for you too, Comrade, not to mention the people, Comrade, and, oh, yes, Comrade, freedom too. But hush . . .)

Jancsi Korom's face was like a girl's back then. We had a short peasant skirt made for him with a thick layer of petticoats and a simple cambric blouse under which, on both sides, he put a round, dry bread roll. Hugging him was 'crisp' as can be. The boys slipped a mischievous hand inside his blouse and ate his two crumbling boobies in public. The tone-setters of the place took our young lady for a whirl repeatedly who, as becomes a blushing virgin, and for another obvious reason, too, kept his dancing partners at bay with his outstretched elbows. But alas, coyness just adds fuel to the spirit of adventure, and before long our young lady came over to our table hissing, 'Better bolt for it!' Which we did.

Once out on the street, he told us that he was fleeing from a buck sergeant who couldn't keep his hands to himself and who insisted on inviting him 'into a nook o' the hall, lass'; then when we reached the first corner he ripped off his wig, jammed his hat on the head of one of the boys, threw his long loden cloak over his shoulder, under which his skirt was rolled up, like a sail out of commission, while his pants, pulled up to the knee, now fell and turned into pantaloons. Just in the nick of time, too! Somebody was running to catch up.

Yes! It was him! The irresistible statesman, his bald pate gleaming like a cow's tits. He caught up with us, running, *our faces stalwart, our fearless hearts a-pounding*; he recognised us, yes, we're the ones, the mates of the little barmaid so dear to his heart; he threw us a grim, searching look, perplexed, agitated, he passed us, hesitated, stopped, and frozen into the likeness of a statue, was soon left behind. Then we heard the thud of his boots as he ran back to the Buzelka, *where is she, where is the girl?*

Well, that's about it. Whereupon the *person in question* lost all his mirth, and that's why we had the Rákosi era. Because of a woman (!). (Which is just another proof of the simple fact that things aren't always what they seem.)

What did he look like?

This story could perhaps be paired with the former. A rural regiment was transferred to Pest. The lads were shown a picture of dear Mátyás, and it was explained to them how to salute 'up front', should they happen to meet the First Secretary's beautiful, Russian-made, golden-wheeled *Chaika*. Only one young Transylvanian lad looked another way, without a glance at the brightly gleaming pate. He must have been thinking about another picture, maybe that of a pretty young girl whom he must now leave, possibly for ever. One of his august superiors spotted the unattending soldier and bawled him out.

'Well, do you know what the First Secretary is like?'

Frightened out of his boots, the private snapped to attention.

'Yes, Sir, I do, Sir!'

'Well?!?'

'Well . . . he's sort'a brown and roundish!'

What happened?
I was scared. (The afternoon of the 16th of June.)

The reflection of truth: a case of overkill
Feri Tsomor, who numbered among the great man's retinue, was known as a devoted swimmer, because that's what he was. His smart uniform stretched proudly across his huge chest. Thanks to his defiantly attractive, photogenic face, he was frequently seen on magazine covers, once by the side of a woman from a textile mill, a Kossuth Prize recipient, and once with a vine grower from Csopak with six 'holds' of land. *Life is nothin' but a bowl a' cherries, work your ass off till you perish*, said those whose eyes came to rest, if only for a moment, on these pictures. On the other hand, it was no child's play, setting up the shots . . .

But not so with Feri Tsomor! His dashing short boots shone like Solomon's balls, his khaki pants had no match in the land, his Russian-style fatigues were a veritable *magnum opus* of the tailor's art, while his small, disc-shaped Society hat, which came with a flat, triangular cap, a so-called *pilotka*, he wore cocked jauntily on the back of his head, which was downy and delicate. He didn't just look like he'd been pulled out of a box, he looked as though inside that box there were eternal sunshine.

Feri Tsomor, he was every editor's dream. Because in order to ensure that that certain quick-witted vine grower with the six 'holds' of land from Csopak shouldn't look like a *kulak*, but shouldn't look like something the cat dragged in either, well, there was more than enough for the reflecting screen, spots and shading gear, all the assorted miracles of technology to attend to. Not to mention the women from the textile mills; they had awkward figures to begin with, and sour faces to boot, as a result of which one had to settle for some sort of abstract and rather vague serenity which those in the know, however, *could* decipher between the lines of the screenplate if they set their minds to it. Even the free and easy laughter that was so much in vogue at the time came out looking inane, more like a sneer, and made the skin of the face strangely thin and drawn and the forehead wholly distasteful, stretched as if it had separated from the top of the heads and the hair-line ... Oh, those foreheads, *flapping in the wind like so many red banners*! Ugh! In one place Ilon Bagits was what Tsomor was in another, bursting with energy, a wool teaser, a sheaf-binder, a schoolgirl, to her it was all the same. She was pretty, young and strong, the girl of our dreams (*cf. Hot stuff*).

Now, then, being responsible for the great man, Feri Tsomor had to take good care of his health. Also, he had to be vigilant. This squat man with the thinning hair who was past his prime lived with the intensity of two; hunting parties, ball games, ring games[11] and other similar pastimes filled his days, and then we haven't even mentioned domestic and foreign policy yet.

One morning, while he was in training and doing the crawl, Tsomor got water in his ear. He jumped up and down on one leg for some time by the side of the pool, but in vain. This is how it must have happened that when during the afternoon's hunt the First Secretary voiced his august wish that what he'd just heard (for someone had just addressed him) he'd like to see

---

[11] A reference to an ancient contest in which one had to grab a ring attached to a pole while riding on horseback (*La Princesse de Clèves*).

directly for himself, our hero thought that his master had expressed interest in a herd.

But that's just it, there wasn't any! Nothing herded together at all! Nothing you could point a decent gun at, anyhow. . . . Since Tsomor did not know what to do, he prayed to the all-powerful and merciful Real to come to his aid; he sent for a lamb, dipped a knife in its throat, and leaving it in to the hilt, he watched with great diligence for any sign of augury, the question being, how much blood would there be and how fast would it flow? What colour would it take on? How quickly would it congeal? How long would the lamb live? How many times would it sigh, and in what manner? As it expired, would it disturb the neat logs under it or, conversely, leave them be?

The signs must have been auspicious, for the orders came popping out as quick and brisk from Tsomor's lips as enamel off of an old pot. His subordinates jumped into their speedy cars and before long many a secret hollow and unsuspected interior was filled with the cowardly lamentations of people he had herded together. (*Thumbscrew:* a press that works by turning a screw. In the Hungarian language, many sayings preserve its memory, the most glaring being, 'he got screwed'. The other is 'long-live [*self-censored*]!' And how about 'all cut up'? And 'cracked up'? What memories do *they* contain? For we make a clear distinction between cutting someone up and cracking a man's skull.)

This was a serious professional blunder.

A match of his own

Ilon Bagits had an older sister. Her name was Veron Bagits, and her thick flaming tresses fluttered down the Váci Road of the forties, that hotbed of Working Class ferment, like a popular ad hoc demonstration. In '46 Veron Bagits defected with a podgy impresario, whereupon in his infinite sadness her fiancé, the heroic István Medve, joined The Force. The story is nevertheless confusing because Veron, who had a lovely voice, appeared as a guest star at an opera performance as early as '49.

Rákosi was in attendance and – I might add – István Medve was not. And this is where it happened that Veron (whose exquisite mound of Venus waxed and waned, stiffened and softened in turn – an exhibition piece if ever there was one!) – sang and played so beautifully, the First Secretary decided to send her a diamond ring as a token of his appreciation. Soon after, our singer requested an audience with the dear man in order to thank him for his thoughtful gift.

The First Secretary was not what you'd call a *bel ami*, but he had plenty of pluck (there had to be a reason, did there not, for why he had got to where he got?) and so the attractive, young and even more plucky diva – for that is what she had become with the help of the fat impresario – in short, the diva began to flirt with the First Secretary, who, being a married man, was taken aback, and turned to the singer of working-class origin with the following words: 'What do you take me for, Comrade? Don't you know I am a married man!'

The little Hungarian working girl with the international experience bowed impertinently. 'Excuse me, dear Mátyás, sweet

Mátyás, I had no idea that Hungarian matches could be lit only on their own boxes . . .'

Clitical exercise
A lady who was faithful to the Working Class Movement backwards and forwards and had turned frigid therein went to see Comrade Rákosi.

'My clitoris!' she yelped like a wounded beast.

'Look! Look at the birdie!' (I can't understand this bird. Sweating every night. And in the morning, its feathers clumpy. I don't even know what kind of bird it is. It neither sings nor hops about. I could make a present of it to someone, but I don't dare. That's my problem. I don't even dare *that*.)

Mother-love
Once, when the dear man went on a journey, a peasant woman in a venerable old village accosted him. She wished to ask him to set free her ruddy-cheeked son because, how should she put it, he hadn't *done* anything.

She began her supplication with these words: 'Good day and may God be with you, dear Mátyás, sweet Mátyás! Let it not displease my lord that I cannot rise up before thee, for the custom of women is upon me. I wish you good health, dear lord. And how is your ladyship's (?!) mother? Is she in good health?'

The First Secretary answered all these questions with his usual meekness, gave the peasant woman salt and *bread* (a great treasure in any village at the time) and a fuzzy cotton seed, and added that until then no son of god had ever inquired after the earthly well-being of his mother.

In two weeks the boy was free! FREE!!!

Fuming mad

In order to protect the interests of the workers and their co-sympathisers the peasants, one fine day the Party decided to raise the price of cigars. ('Dear, dear, all those phlegmatic, brownish, nicotine-tainted spittles,' came the verdict from the upper echelons by way of disapproval.) At this a multitude of representatives surrounded the First Secretary, and not a few complaints could be heard pertaining to the subject.

'Dear Mátyás, sweet Mátyás, if things go on like this we shall all have to give up smoking. And that wouldn't do at all!' whined the sulking elders of the state. But looking over the line of men of working-class origin armed to the teeth with thick, fuming cigars and flashing the ironic smile that never missed its mark, Rákosi merely said, 'You just go on *fuming*, gentlemen.' Then he walked out on the outwitted company. Ever since, these characteristic words are on everyone's lips: *You just go on fuming, gentlemen.*

You get what you pay for

On the occasion of an exciting Central Committee coffee klatch, one of the spokesmen for democratic self-censorship launched a merciless attack upon himself, the object of which was the over-zealousness of the state security organs. He further commented that he was nursing individuals of unsatisfactory expertise on his bosom.

Hearing this, Rákosi merely said, for the jobs like *these* for pay like *this*, what do you expect? Bishops? Upon which the comrade who had made the interpolation smiled and declared a cease-fire upon himself.

My [self-censored] itches like the dickens, I'm gonna [self-censored] it soon as it [self-censored]

On the occasion of yet another exciting Central Committee coffee klatch, Mátyás had to read out a transcript that had come from Higher Quarters to the East. But as he was about to launch into it, he inadvertently touched that part of his anatomy (it was itching) with which one usually doesn't think. Meanwhile, he was already saying, 'Comrades, they sent us a missive!' At which someone shouted out, 'That's not where they sent it, Matyi!' At which János Barcsi-Balogh added, *'but that's where it belongs!'*

The solution

For some unfathomable reason *plus* the assiduous undercover activities of the Imperialists, Rákosi began to slip down the popularity list. Since he was just about to attend a peace rally, the officials in charge wanted to ensure that the great man's welcome should be as warm and enthusiastic as humanly possible. It fell to Minister of Transport Comrade Gerő to ask the popular writer Tibor Déry[12] to come up with a plan for the reception. It

---

[12] Déry (1896–1977): generally regarded as the finest writer of socialist prose. But his political activities immediately before and after 1956 created much friction.

shouldn't cost much, it should take the First Secretary by surprise, while the people, too, should be pleased.

Déry, who liked to do things in a big way whatever the situation, gave a reluctant shrug and said, 'I can't think of anything.' After a while, though, he added, 'Well, perhaps I can.' His eyes sparkling with hope and anticipation, Gerő urged him on: 'Well? Well?'

'Will dear Mátyás have himself driven over the bridge?'

'*Da.*' [*trans. from the Russian: Yes.*]

'Past the two pillars at the head of the bridge?'

'*Da. Da.*' [*trans. from the Russian: Yes. Yes.*]

'In that case, have Mihály Farkas hanged on one pillar and yourself on the other. It won't cost much, the dear man will be surprised, and the people will be deliriously happy.' With that he grabbed his hat and walked out.

Whether this exchange really took place or not I cannot say. But that it was on everyone's lips and that every Hungarian was glad to hear it is as sure as I stand here.

Hot stuff
Once there lived a *real woman* by the name of Ilon Bagits. But one fine day, her radiant youthfulness and endearing dimples disappeared from the magazine covers, never again to stand as living proof that the working class, the sympathising peasantry,

the progressive intelligentsia, not to mention the peoples' police, arm and arm and all that jazz.

Just as the capitalists have wiped and indeed continue to wipe the optimistic smile off the face of the working class in the given historical situation, so did said smile disappear from the lips of Ilon Bagits.

What happened?

What happened is that there came into being a very *fine*, exclusive government resort, the kind of place where those who entered became as fair as the very angels, where the trees yielded bright stars instead of fruit, silvery springs trickled under their leafy boughs, and snow-white doves sang songs of enchantment. Even the crowing of the crow sounded as sweet as the trill of the nightingale, and every gypsy girl was an angel. A golden lion stood guard, and in the glittering rooms of the nationalised fairy-tale palace ringed with golden shrubs, the guests sat on golden benches and ate golden ducks, golden geese and golden oxen with golden knives and golden forks served up by the common folk dressed in golden livery. Thus did the people's republic hope to show a token of its appreciation to those who stood up for its interests so faithfully. (I stood up to it myself.)

On the fine, sandy stretch of beach by the shore it was the custom to bathe in the buff, but not in order to parade one's sexuality in an irresponsible and bourgeois manner as certain dogmatic comrades contended in an offensive manner, but because it *felt good*. They were happy to have the blessed sun warm their most secret regions; the men took pleasure in the naked women, and the women in the naked men. The rest was sour grapes. There was a brief transitional period characterised by a bit of confusion, I admit. But things eventually fell into their proper place, not to mention the fact that the detractors must have forgotten about the meticulous theoretical training of those who disported themselves in this paradise. Which was adding insult to injury.

Since I can speak with the authority of the eyewitness who feels a sentimental yearning for my own lost youth, I can safely say that I was a little uneasy at the innocence with which we examined each other's privates, boobs, and what not. It brought Jaspers to mind, *innocence is ignorance*. Because I had no wish to flatter myself by thinking that I was any worse or any more decadent than the others, I found this *pretentious naturalness* suspect. All the same, I enjoyed it, the physicality, the water, the sun, the smell of the other bodies – but above all the women, to let the cat out of the bag.

I had a favourite rock, a petrus of my very own, which reached into the water so tentatively that it made the huge, aggressive monster seem ingratiatingly *tenuous*. In my unbounded arrogance I was practically *loath* to step on it. Since the rock was facing east, I spent many a long morning on top of it meditating with legs flung apart, exposing my groin to the sun. Delicious. And in the evening after the sun had set and that black comrade darkness made its cautious appearance, I'd give free rein to the natural urge to piss into the water in a great arch. The boundless water was at my feet and at a distance, a distance so great it hardly needed to be taken into account at all, was the indistinct conjoining of sea and sky, while more or less across from all this, much closer, I felt the rough rock under my feet; I'd have liked to cling to it monkey-like, me and my kind, *angel and ape*, the sole of the foot twitching, the twitching zigzagging up to the groin, for a moment disrupting the arch of the urine, *it's done*, but then there's more! more! and in this delirious moment the mind, overwhelmed, conceives of the distant, gentle splashing as a continuous train of thought which links man to the universe.

A woman can have no idea what it is like.

The resort was sequestered from the outside world by a high wire fence, but in order to add a touch of class to the act of admission, the management came up with a mighty refined idea. Thumbing their noses at the picayune objective difficulty spring-ing from the fact that it had no ocean, the guests were brought to the resort grounds via an ocean liner. *There was a big cement tub filled with salt water and a boat fixed in place.* Lots of fun and frolic, as you can imagine.

The helmsman charged a nominal fee for taking us across. A priggish sea lion with gold teeth, Branko was his name. He had a penchant for practical jokes, he called his sea a Potemkin sea, all show and no substance, and he liked to pat the women's *sterns*, who giggled when he whispered in their ears by way of consolation, 'Potemkin? Never you mind, mam, don't you fret, we'll do a number on it anyhow!' This man Branko was like a great military commander who loved to cop a feel; deadly calm, with a calmness that came from the guts, and he *knew* something, besides. (During Tito's show trials his boat was made good use of, to say the least.) Branko thumbed his nose at the official schedule of events sent from Moscow, adorned with so many red stars that it caused not a little difficulty in the deciphering (from whence to where, summer and winter schedules, and so on). He'd take off when a sufficient number of people had gathered.

'Dearies,' he grinned, 'there ain't enough of you yet, but just you wait.'

Its front 'plumb like 'em south-German womenfolk' (Branko), the boat was no state of the art, to say the least. Still, when we kicked off and Branko revved up the Johnson (it was still a Johnson then, only later did they bring a local variety from Kuybishev which to be perfectly honest wasn't bad, though it wasn't *entirely* satisfactory either); the boat reared up like a proud stallion, and as we tore through the water, our bright and shiny manes flapped howling in the invigorating wind; and if at such times we sank our hands into the water, a mist shrouded the boat. Pierced by the strong, bright sunlight that was so much a part of our sea, it was like an ornate tent painted in the myriad bright colours of the rainbow. 'The old Horthy regime had nothing like it!' we said gleefully as our eyes sparkled with the old serenity (*cf. The misery of the small east-european nations*).

With time the passengers of the boat became friendly, but I saw that they (myself included) were casting *furtive glances* at each other, looking people not in the eye, *en garde!* or trivially at the groins, but at the curve of a shoulder, inside the tunnel of a wide-sleeved shirt, or at a mysteriously disappearing and reappearing elbow.

In the eternal sunshine Branko had gotten a deep tan which was different from our *campaign brown*, attractive as it may have been; his face was weathered by the salt and sea air, his flaxen hair flapped in the never-ending silent breeze; on the trip back he sometimes executed a jolly good honour lap, distending his belly, saluting ceremoniously, which those on the landing stage acknowledged by an enthusiastic wave of the hand. At such times the breasts of the women are more lovely than ever, and quiver, too. (A man: 'When Ilon stands over me on all fours the domes of her breasts hang down, down, she wiggles her rear end vigorously, her boobs dangle, her pubic hair juts out between her legs, and she throws an enigmatic shadow on the wall.') At deboarding he again copped a feel when and where he could and said as if to no one in particular, *I destroy, I destroy, I destroy . . .'*

I think he scorned our nudity, and he spoke to us with the superiority peculiar to servants. (Was he trying to tell us that we are the ruling class?) He was fond of saying 'it is best to cut a long story short,' nor did he ever answer the riddle about the difference between a *lot* of water and the sea, he just shrugged; he was also fond of saying 'every trembling bush doth sigh,' then sighed deeply, as if he were a trembling bush himself. He pulled off his worn silesia pants just once ('not right for a man o' the sea, the sea'll get sore); he had a huge ∼, only the balls betraying his age, if at all; we men slapped him on the back as if he had done well by us, while giggling, the women turned to each other, 'I should have it so good . . .' Then later, during the show trials, Branko came to a tragic end. For which there is no excuse. (Ever since, the newly assigned guests stumble across the bone-dry cement tub cursing – and cowed, too, by its horrendous futility . . .)

Like Ilon Bagits, Gyurka Nagy, the nationally known director of a factory, was also among the regulars. This brawny man who had been lifted out and up from the life of a simple lathe hand remained the working-class Angel's Ground rough-neck he had always been. At first he'd leave a meeting without so much as a how-dee-do and run down to the *sweatshop* to *put his back into it*. 'I miss it,' he shrugged when he was cautiously questioned about it. But then he thought better of it, it's not what a director should be concerned with, until gradually he brought to his management of the factory the pluck based on brains, ambition and individual talent that he picked up by the shore of the Rákos Stream in his native district. The times were not yet ripe for it, but that's another story.

Suffice it to say, in the early morning Gyurka Nagy took to jogging along the shore. The sun burned him something awful; the very first day he looked like a gypsy. He had been given the nickname of Charcoal many years before. Once Elemér Orbán, who had just fallen out of favour and who sailed through the factory yard with the spry but nervous gait of the fallen, called to Gyurka Nagy, who stood within the ornamental ring of a couple of comrades from the Ministry. 'Hiyya, Charcoal! What the f . . . are you doing in this bawdy house?' Gyurka Nagy released himself from the neat ring of his peers, slapped his old chum on the back, and with a loud chuckle said, *'I'm the madame!'*

He was so dark that if anyone caught a glimpse of his lean, muscular body on a white sheet, their eyes were dazzled by the sight. To which we should add (i.e., to the bedazzlement) that Gyurka was also the proud owner of a huge ~; we men slapped him on the back as if he had done well by us, while giggling, the women turned to each other, 'I should have it so good . . .' Enmeshed by a wild growth of thick, swelling veins like so many mistletoes that held it in thrall, it was strong and wide like a haycock's. Common parlance, but especially experience, has come to distinguish two kinds of ~, the wiener ~ and the wham-danger ~. Though the reference is clear, it is not meant to be judgemental, not even in intimate woman-to-woman talk, it's

merely the way things stand, though without a doubt the wiener
~ is surrounded by some sort of (unmerited) awe; a pardonable
error, after all, you can't be *sure*, it might *grow*. In short, the
wiener ~ is regarded as a *large hunk* of wham-danger ~. And
Gyurka Nagy had a classical wiener ~.

The enchanted woodland of planted pines was interspersed with
wooden bungalows of the domestic Hungarian and Czech import
variety. In one of these was lodged Gyurka Nagy, in another Ilon
Bagits. I should also mention Gyurka Nagy's terrible awakenings.
He woke to the break of day with something like animal fear, at
first whimpering like an infant, then screaming and shouting so
loud and in such an incredibly strident and hysterical manner
that for some time the guards were regularly alerted. Only very
gradually did everyone calm down.

Except Ilon Bagits, that is. Because from then on she got up
with Gyurka Nagy, pressed her forehead (and not some *flapping*
forehead, mind!) to the cool windowpane, watching the water
and scratching herself lazily, the way peculiar to women in the
early hours of the morning. Our story will soon come to an end.
The lake still had that special light that a tourist or native today
would look for in vain.

'The back of the water,' Ilon whispered, then strolled out to the
lake butt-naked where she watched the rising sun, the 'back of
the water', and she shivered in the misty chill of the early
morning. Gyurka Nagy was jogging along the deserted beach.
From time to time he sprinted into the shallow water as unselfconscious as a puppy, making sand and water fly. A shadow like
a black tongue of flame flitted past Bagits, the huge something
swinging between Gyurka's legs like an *emancipated* beast – an

awful shade! (Inadvertently one thought, whose? And what sort of fear is this, we would have asked each other, had we not been afraid.)

For some time Ilon watched Gyurka, who took no notice of her, until his naked butt disappeared among the light dunes. The next day Bagits joined him without saying a word; for his part he picked up his pace as if attempting to shake her off, but Ilon would not relent, though she could barely keep up. Then they both began to sweat and gasp for air. When they reached the shrubs by the fence − the traces of Gyurka Nagy's wild turn-abouts were clearly visible in the loose sand − still without uttering a single word, nothing but the sweating and the gasping for air, they fell on each other. *Good*, said Gyurka Nagy. *Good*, said Ilon Bagits. Which is as much as they ever said to each other in all their lives.

What with the photographers piddling about all day trying to capture the awesome though well-intentioned grins of the women from the textile mills, Ilon's promotion went up in smoke. 'I'm not sorry. I shall never be sorry as long as I live,' she said. Gyurka Nagy said nothing.

Come on baby light my fire, II
It was a bitterly cold winter in '52 or thereabouts, when on a freezing, windy January day two personality culters were driving back to Budapest. When the road took them past the gypsy tents located along the Roman Baths just outside of town, they caught a glimpse of an old gypsy who was indolently puffing on his pipe, watching the road from behind the opening of one of the tents. In order to demonstrate that the leaders and the led are

birds of a feather, one of the comrades called to the old gypsy, 'Bitter cold, ain't it, old man?' 'You should know,' the old gypsy countered, 'you're the one on the outside.'

Once there lived, I

Once there lived a man from the ÁVÓ. He was a lonely, withdrawn man who, unless duty called, would not leave his home for days. He'd sit quietly daydreaming in his armchair, reading profusely and taking ample notes, and when the mood was on him, he would put on his best overcoat and with a heavy yet cheerful heart stroll down to the nearby Danube, by the old ferry landing.

At first he pitched round pebbles into the water, watching the concentric rings with satisfaction; then, when he got bored, he took some flat pebbles and played ducks and drakes, a game in which he was something of an expert. After a while this bored him too, and then he resumed his walk, engaging in pleasantries with the house owners along the shore, chatting about the weather, the mosquitoes, the water level. Be bought fried *lángos*, because they put green pepper rings and sliced tomatoes on top, which he loved and couldn't get anyplace else. He complimented the ladies, handing them stolen lilacs with an impish smile. This bit of ambiguity felt good, you could tell. Then taking a slight detour, he made his way home.

From time to time his friends would pay him a visit, which pleased him no end. They would go sit out on the terrace, the guest in the creaking wicker chair and he on the uncomfortable wooden stool which, however, he did not feel was uncomfortable (not so his behind!). This allowed him to sit hunched at his guest's feet with the vanity and peculiar superiority of the disciple until nightfall, when the mosquitoes forced them inside.

For her part, his neighbour, an ageless, priceless creature, always brought him something to nibble on; from exquisite creations with mayonnaise to rustic breads of all sorts they'd nibble away the afternoon, but without stuffing themselves. On the contrary. They felt a light, devil may care, slightly *aggressive* hunger and couldn't wait for the evening's surprise, which was no other than some sort of pumpkin dish made according to the secret policeman's very own recipe. But which? Well, that was the surprise! The best was the dish seasoned with marjoram. But there was one with dill, another with golden cress, still another prepared the Hungarian way, and who knows how many others!

These afternoons were peaceful, tranquil and good, and if there remained an ounce of bitterness in the secret policeman's heart when his guest parted, there was surely no helping it, and it meant only that something had come to an end that had to come to an end.

'*Leave-taking is a little like dying*,' a departing guest once remarked. The secret policeman pricked up his ears. He knew he was living in a world where anything might happen, but he had no idea that this *anything* could be his friend. 'You don't understand,' the other said quickly. And truly, that's just how it was. 'The day before yesterday I got scared [*self-censored*] because while I was at work, your name was mentioned in such a *tentative* tone of voice. And you know what this sort of tentative tone of voice bodes these days.' The secret policeman smiled behind his moustache. 'Don't give it a second thought, old boy!'

Sometimes, during the course of a long afternoon, probably from the strong, oblique rays of the sun, he would get a racking headache. His eyes played him false, and he pressed his eyeballs repeatedly as if in an attempt to grab hold of the pain. But sleep would invariably make it disappear, and he considered this a sign of grace –

Once there lived, II

Once there lived a man from the ÁVÓ who was as legendary for his stinginess as he was for his undying devotion to the Party.

With the help of the crude quality control system in effect at the time, he nevertheless managed to bring these two contradictory psychological states of mind into harmony by keeping a *bulging* statue of Stalin on the table adjacent to his desk into which he'd throw the money that came his way from where he sat. During his sleight of hand, though, a portion of the money would *inevitably* fall to the side.

Before leaving for the day, he would tally the contents of the statue with his written accounts, never failing to give vent to his bewilderment: how the *dickens* did all that money end up on this table? Then, as he calmly swept up the solid new forints he'd say, 'And why not? Have I not given the king his due?'

Blue funk

Our bright winds were still a-blowin' (it was the late forties and the giant import ventilator had not yet been shut off!) when near the Pagan Tower in Csillaghegy the president of the city council was celebrating his name day. (His Christian name was

Ferenc, but he celebrated it on Peter-Paul's, that's how vigilant he was.) In his folksy, hospitable home he welcomed among the local notables a lieutenant from the ÁVÓ whose inexhaustible fount of humour was the stuff of legend.

After dinner, the lieutenant patted the file of papers sticking out of his pocket. 'Now then, gentlemen-comrades, here comes the *pièce de résistance!*' he said, and pulling the unfamiliar bit of paper out (about cow breeding in America and the delicate seasoning of Serbian dishes), he offered them around with his usual loquacity. The comrades tasted the rare titbits with appreciation, liberally praising the style, the choice of words, never suspecting that the moustachioed lieutenant who had joined in the extravagant analytical praise had a cruel joke up his sleeve.

The next day, in the grey, numbing dawn, two ÁVÓ officers dressed in their best uniforms asked to be admitted. Startled awake from his dreams, the president of the city council thought he could discern a causal relationship between the early-morning visit of the secret police and the papers he had received the night before and so, in his fright (because fear had pressed its ugly ass up against the nation), before admitting his visitors the poor man quickly consigned his rare treasures to the flames.

Head bowed, the council president stood over the papers disappearing in the fire. Aged and annihilated, he felt a pressure in his chest as if his bronchial tubes were filled with some very weighty matter. He had trouble breathing and his lips were suddenly chapped, but at the same time a whitish coat of spittle appeared in the corners; his fingers ran down his ashen cheeks, and he was horrified to discover that his carefully shaven face had grown a stubble; the lines were deep cavities, while the bones had shifted their places – or so it seemed. Could it be his past as a social democrat, he reflected, with its shaky bourgeois code of morals tainted with a leftist colouring? When he raised a hand to his eyes he felt something sticky, but he could not cry. His nostrils quivered, *the smell of old age*, he could almost feel the molecules decompose. 'I am old,' he said out loud. His teeth clicked as he closed his lips. The black cinders stirred.

Meanwhile, in accordance with their orders, the meek young ÁVÓ officers infiltrated the place, saluted sprucely, and in the name of the division wished their dear Ferenc, their sweet comrade, good health and happiness on his esteemed name day. *You are my sunshine!*

Will you settle . . .?

The butcher János Besze was blessed with the strongest voice of any of the available civilian spokesmen. When he spoke the walls would shake to their foundations. Hoping to capitalise on Besze's outstanding qualities as an orator, the Executive Committee for the Year of Transmission [*sic!*] asked, would he kindly address the spontaneous Independence Day gathering assembled at the steps of the National Museum?

At the decisive moment Besze, eager to oblige, stood at the top of the steps. His red nose shone into the far distance, and his humble check shirt, which he would not part with for weeks on end, billowed in the wind. Then he let out a mighty roar. *Will you settle for slavery?* he intoned, which is all the eager crowd needed to hear who, not waiting for the rest, thundered in unison, *Yes we will! Yes we will!* And with that his speech was at an end.

Don't!

A sad Magyar world it was back in the fifties, but the young, because that's what the young are like, that vehement, that sweet, that reckless, that amorous, that fragile? would nevertheless occasionally give themselves over to a bit of tearful merrymaking. This is what they did at the House of Culture out in Csillaghegy once, during a dance.

The gypsy was playing a foreign, internationalist tune, whereupon one of the young people stopped him.

'Hang it all, play something Hungarian!'

Hearing this, the old comrade Pál Korniss, who had veritably wasted away from witnessing the many infractions of the law, the personality cult, the disappointment over what had become of his childhood dream, his twenty years of perseverance and dedication – anyway, he jumped up on top of the table and with tears coming to his eyes, he shouted at the gypsy, 'Don't do it, man! *There's been more than enough hanged already!*'

The wager

The Beke family has died out. The last Beke, who lived near the Stalin Bridge, was a distinguished, well-to-do bachelor. He also had a formidable appetite and loved to entertain. ('Beke's bolting it down,' his acquaintances would say squinting encouragingly at the sight of such a *whole lot* of food, while his colleagues, when the nimble wind brought the sound of human wailing from some distant quarter, would nod knowingly, 'Beke's boltin' it to somebody again.' But later, when Beke had to bolt for it himself and was caught, drawn and quartered into the bargain, it caused so much pain all around that the word-play petered out like a poorly attended fire.) Beke dragged the working men he found on his rounds (*ex*: the shipyard) to his home almost by force, but whoever accepted his cordial invitation found a tenacious welcome. Besides, having no issue of any kind or collateral descendants, Hungary and the Comecon inherited his entire fortune!

Anyway, they were sitting at lunch once, eating an ingenious meal of cooked squash with breaded aubergine, when an ÁVÓ officer appeared and without so much as a how-dee-do grabbed a chair, pulled the dish over to him and dug in like the devil. His face was soon glistening with fat (there was some bacon fat left over from the day before; warmed up, it was poured over the squash seasoned with golden cress). Beke and his guests just stared at the ÁVÓ officer. When he was well into his squash, Beke said to him, 'Where did'ya come in, friend?'

'Through the gate, where else?!' the latter said, stuffing it in, confident in his mission – a by-product of his privileged position, which was further bolstered by the knowledge that wherever he and his kind appeared (factories, workshops, offices and ministries, farmers' co-ops, state co-ops, consumers' co-ops, the street, company dances and family gatherings) people shuddered, the conversation died down, and everyone looked apprehensively at everyone else. The concept of hatred was not unfamiliar to him.

'Think you could come in again?' Beke asked calmly, adding after a mischievous pause, 'provided I were to let you out?'

'Sure thing!'

'Well, friend, if you can come in a second time, you can have your pick of the best medal in my collection, though they're so beautiful, old Stakhanovite Ignác Pióker would give his eye-tooth for them!'[13]

'You're on,' said the ÁVÓ officer.

They finished lunch. The officer was asked to leave, whereupon Beke unleashed his four terrifying draggle-tailed sheep dogs. Then he shouted to the policeman waiting beyond the gate. (And we know what waiting will do. It makes you immoral.) 'Okay, you can come in now!'

The ÁVÓ officer opened the gate and as he did so, he quickly pulled his round, flat Society hat over his eyes, dropped on all fours and began tottering and grunting through his nose in a most peculiar manner. When the four dogs set eyes on the grotesque figure, they took off like the devil was after them.

The crafty ÁVÓ officer won the best medal in the collection, which afterwards Beke bought back with lots of shiny forints amidst hearty laughter.

What's the problem?
Comrade Attila F. had a difficult nature and a cunning sort of brain besides, and so, when the local peasants were told to band into a farmers' co-op, they couldn't see eye to eye with him.

---

[13] Which was a lot of teeth, considering that a conscientious Stakhanovite, a worker who had gone over the production quota set by the State, had more than enough medals of his own already. Being a celebrated Stakhanovite, Ignác Pióker certainly had his fair share.

They were, how shall I put it, veritably in awe of his brain. Having grown ashamed of this himself, once the old ÁVÓ officer turned to the peasants, pleading with them as follows: 'My sons! Why won't you see eye to eye with me? Didn't I always want what is best for you?'

Whereupon an old peasant shouted, 'That's just it, sweet Attila, sweet Comrade! You never *would* settle for less!'

Poetry and reality

Our young ÁVÓ officers, who, due to the constraints of the barracks system, must often share a room amongst themselves (penetrating male odours, the simple, perverse games of the fraternity, sleepless nights and so forth), play many a practical joke on each other in those precious free hours when they can give vent to their impish spirits.

Some of the unmarried ÁVÓ officers from Újpest managed to get hold of a couple of canaries which canaries, however, wouldn't sing for love or money. They were as silent as the grave. So after a while the disappointed owners soon passed the tiny creatures off. Anyway, one of the tight-lipped canaries wandered from owner to owner until a man by the name of Péter Karmazsin bought it for a nominal sum. (*Nota bene*, he was the one who loved painting on glass so much, and who, having gotten hold of some enormous plates, adorned them with such huge penises, people came from as far as Kiev to admire them.) His comrades teased him no end for keeping such a bird, such a sad stool pigeon. He wouldn't fetch a farthing for him, not until silence would be really golden.

Anyway, in the spirit of fun, they bought two candy eggs the size of canary eggs and placed one in the cage. Having returned from an exhausting stint of duty, the unsuspecting Karmazsin jumped for joy, forgetting in a flash the early-morning nuisance and vexation that were part of his profession, and from then on looked after his bird with more loving care than ever.

The next day there were two eggs! His joy knew no bounds. 'Wow! Two eggs!' he said. 'Which means I can expect two more canaries. I shall get a handsome sum for their song and make a respectable profit.' (Though let it be said in favour of the Corps that the bird also got taken for a ride in so far as it sat patiently trying to hatch them.)

After a while the 'conspirators' (which must be understood in quotes, *cf. The conspiracy*) went a step further, and on the Soviet ship that was anchored in the harbour, where you could buy anything from Hungarian *Matyó* dolls through hussars and jack knives, they bought two tiny fake wooden nestling birds. (The Soviet sailors laughed wholeheartedly when they learned about the ruse . . .)

Returning from duty in the wee hours of the morning, drenched to the bone, exhausted, his cheeks ashen, nothing to write home about, I can tell you, obscurely betrayed by the room, the secret policeman greeted the tiny arrivals with glee, while in his mind's eye he was already jingling the melodious forints he'd be receiving for them.

Then, as if he were a professional bird breeder, he went in search of a nest. Having returned with the small bread-basket-type nest, he carefully set to work so that he could move the diminutive factors of his financial future into their new home. But as he picked up the little panting things (theoretically, at least), he couldn't help but take a closer look.

'Well I'll be dangled!'

Our friend from the ÁVÓ couldn't make head or tail of it. Then in a flash the wool fell from his eyes and looking over the line of his friendly comrades, who were choking with laughter, he roared like a wounded beast, 'Who is responsible for this?!'

Needless to say, no one would admit to the mischief even though our friend reasoned that anyone who had the nerve to think it up should also have the nerve to own up to it. In his justified outrage he grabbed the innocent little nestlings and flung them out of the window. Go with God's blessing! And off they flew . . . (I can't understand this bird. Sweating every night. And in the morning, its feathers clumpy. I don't even know what kind of bird it is. It neither sings nor hops about. I could make a present of it to someone, but I don't care. That's my problem, that I don't even dare do *that*.)

Let us come to grief!
Master Gedeon Magyar was blessed with more than his fair share of peasant cunning. When spring came (*nastupilo oseny!*) and the old corn needed turning over, this crafty man had a devilish idea. He decided to outsmart the authorities. But as we shall see, the authorities outsmarted him instead.

Anyway, he decided to send an anonymous denunciation to the

authorities which said that there was a considerable quantity of *** hidden under the corn in Gedeon Magyar's granary.

The authorities came, offered their greetings, shovelled through the corn – and found nothing. At which the peasant, who had been watching the entire manoeuvre with the utmost composure, thanked the 'gentlemen' for their 'thoughtfulness' and offered them a bit o' wine to wash down the dust that was stuck in their throats. The 'gentlemen' thanked him wryly, then hurried away from the scene of their humiliation.

A paleface never forgets, and when months later one of the secret policemen, who was dressed in his civvies, met a man selling ***, he had an idea. He told the man to deliver the *** to the Magyar farm but without saying why, or who sent him.

That same afternoon they showed up, and the ÁVÓ officer in question said to the peasant, who was understandably taken aback at this repeated visit, 'There was a mistake made last time, Comrade. But we shall rectify it.'

Our man, who was too smart by half for his own good, scratched the back of his head where the wounds had nicely healed, with only a couple of bald spots standing as reminders of the time that had passed. 'Well,' he said after he'd paid his dues and had sat out every one of his gaol sentences, 'well, it may not be such a bright idea after all *starting up* with them.'

Done in proper

Poor István Medve! It is safe to say that he, too, was also hard hit by that whoreson of an era. After Veron Bagits had walked out on him, a profound sadness settled on his soul. He had his hair cropped short, which made his face look round, and his walnut-brown eyes sat deep in the hollow of their sockets like in some profound bottomless well. 'Sadness comes *oozing* out of Pista like piss from a piss hole,' his friends said whenever he would abruptly excuse himself from company and hurry home, or when a good friend, because of the intimacy he could assume existed between them, refused to be tactful with him, whereupon in sad, matter-of-fact tones, he'd use his fluctuating blood-sugar level as an excuse.

He conjured up before the mind's eye the friendly pressure of Veron's right arm, the melodious ringing of her voice, the encouraging twinkle in her merry eye, her ingratiating smile, and he conjured up too the profound conversations when István thought he had said everything, but then Veron began to question him softly, using short, simple sentences, that's what her questions were like, from which it soon appeared that István had not told her everything after all. The words contained in the questions and comments penetrated the shady nooks and crannies of what had previously been said, and Veron launched into an explanation; she explained what István saw and why he saw what he saw the way he saw it. (What a *coincidence* that the literary gentleman Sándor Gergely[14] should have happened to feel *exactly* the same way about Mátyás Rákosi – the pressure, the melodious ringing, the cheer, the simple sentences, the shady nooks, what and why, all! all! – In short, life is beautiful and fantastic, lovely and sacred; fine, we thumb our noses; they can do as they like, the world is still a much better place and life is still much more

[14] Gergely was president of the State-supervised Hungarian Writers Union, but never mind.

special than what it would appear to be with a sober mind. Though I would not call it *real*; that would be stretching things a bit.)

Sad and forlorn, he wandered through our city's meandering streets very like a beam of moonlight. But what becomes a beam of moonlight does not become Pista Medve! His wide shoulder pads brushed against the house walls and gradually wore away. Horrible! You can imagine it for yourselves. His shoulder straps also started fraying at the seams. He couldn't even let himself go during the great communal bacchanalia (*ex*: compulsory produce delivery). Once the dear man himself turned to Pista with a question pertaining to this.

'What's up, youth-a'-the-nation, why ain't we dancin'?'

'I *ain't* got the *heart.*'

For a moment Rákosi was taken aback, but then he went up to Medve and said softly and soberly, 'It is not right, Comrade. We have learned to work. We must now learn to play!'

And so Medve gave it his all. Day after day he sat at the upper end of a T-shaped table as the dear man's encouragement buzzed in his ears – all this amid the heaving billows of disappointed love! No wonder Pista Medve took to drink . . . But not any old kind either! He drank of the water of speechifying, the glass of water that was reserved specially for orators! (The country is being built and beautified, and the like. It's coming out at our ears.)

He gulped it down with such despairing passion, such disappointed gusto, you'd think it was a glass of vodka. At first he reached for the glass by sidling up to it, trying to keep up appearances, his fingers advancing along the red table-cloth, sliding along the folds or over the pale stains; thus did the poor man hope, with recourse to the logic of geometry, to authenticate the mad forays of his fingers. He played with the glass as if they had no serious designs on each other. His hand edged along the rim, and so forth. But in a flash the easy style was gone, and István Medve's hand fastened like a noose (!) around the glass, and he gulped it down!

With time the all too human vacillation was gone. The committee hadn't even settled in their seats when István had already gotten his glass by the throat. But addiction knows no bounds, and Medve too got carried away. Also, truth to tell, he would from time to time fling his glass over his shoulder, which would go crash-bang against the life-size portraits, *long live Lenin! long live Stalin! long live Rákosi!* and before long the committee itself would have been splashed in the face and whatnot. But just then the problem was solved, because Medve was, to speak plainly, *done in.*

The conspiracy

Rajk[15] was done in too, and possibly this was the doing in that did most to obliterate all hopes for our New Age . . .

The conspiracy was exposed by Rajk's maid, who discovered it in a most surprising manner.

[15] First name still László. The rest in footnote 8.

One evening she was alone in Rajk's apartment when all of a sudden, out of pure boredom, she felt an irresistible urge to try on her master's best suit. When she had it on she stood in front of the mirror admiring herself, because she was the kind of woman who likes to see herself in men's clothing. But then, to her horror, she heard footsteps. It was the minister, come home in the company of his friends.

Not wishing to bring the anger of her kind master down upon her head, the frightened girl tried to flee, but it was too late. She then hid under the bed, and not a moment too soon! Rajk and Co. entered the room to conspire late into the night.

The very next day the maid, who had heard every word, ran in a frenzy to denounce the dangerous band of conspirators.

The apple of his eye

István Medve was no spring chicken when he decided to give himself eight days off to visit his aged parents. And what a to-do there was, what rejoicing! His mother cooked and baked with special loving care; she even made her son's favourite, scones with cracklings. A couple of days into his visit, though, István Medve thought he could discern *certain forbidden thoughts* behind his father's words, and in keeping with regulations, put these down for the record.

After he had finished, and with the satisfaction that comes from work well done, he hurried to headquarters, where in accordance with regulations, he submitted a written report to his superiors. This courageous and noble act was exceptionally well received considering the escalating (?) international (?) situation (?), and

Medve was short-listed as 'an especially conscientious and reliable lamb who has returned to the fold', whereupon he soon surpassed all his comrades in stature.

What *really* happened though, was this. The whole thing had been planned in advance. The boy unveiled his plan and his loving parent was more than happy to make the sacrifice. They spent many a sweltering afternoon out in the barn practising what he'd say, because the boy, not wishing to trust anything to chance and afraid of being bugged himself, wished to reveal the forbidden matter in a *real* conversation. In the end, this slightly obscene but highly efficacious campaign of self-promotion hardly cost him anything (food and lodging, plus the crackling scones). But his aim – his aim was accomplished!

Who discovered Dániel Berzsenyi?

On account of some concrete event that was posing a grave threat to the nation, in the lieutenant-colonel's absence his deputy had certain slips of paper hurriedly printed announcing that it was forbidden for those who had been relocated or were about to be relocated[16] to make friendly overtures to the ÁVÓ officers who might be dropping in on them for a cordial chat. They were further warned not be attempt to delineate the course of their lives in any personal manner, or with bourgeois-humanistic brush-strokes to attempt to hide their pernicious, oppressive leanings, to play cards (RED takes it!), or even to chat, *interrupto*, about literature, art, and love. These posters were put up in the

[16] After the Communist takeover in 1949, aristocrats and diplomats, doctors and lawyers, teachers and engineers, shop-keepers and tinkers, tailors and candle-stick makers were rounded up and taken to distant farms where, if they were lucky, they got to work in the fields in exchange for food.

homes of the enemies of the working class, mostly in the so-called *salon*, which was usually just a small protuberance of an oversized hall, or a corner of the veranda.

The ÁVÓ officers were mightily annoyed that due to the less than immaculate behaviour of their more immature, sometimes *psychologically perverted* comrades, they were thus put to shame. But despite all their blushing protestations, as long as the decree was in effect, their hands were tied.

Then one fine day the lieutenant-colonel decided to take a little side-trip to study the effective implementation of the above-mentioned relocations of the perfidious enemies of the working class. When he finished his business he washed his hands, and animated by the mild yet lovely autumn weather, he had himself driven back in a buggy. However, in order to pass the time (because he was piqued when it did *not pass*) he decided to try his hand at a crossword puzzle. As he was passing a vineyard by the side of the road, however, he noticed two men toiling by the press-shed, two simple country bumpkins conversing now in French, now in English, and now in Austrian-accented German. Imperialistic languages, of course! And so he stopped the carriage in order to conduct an identity check.

Since he had found everything in order, but just a moment before had a problem with 54 down, he turned to one of the two men. 'Excuse me, sir,' he began in a graciously apt style, 'could you kindly tell me who discovered Dániel Berzsenyi *back then*?'[17]

---

[17] Berzsenyi (1776–1836): the great pre-Romantic poet, one of whose main themes was the concern with the decay of the individual, the other with the decay of the nation. '*Back then*': a reference to the awful, unspeakable times before the triumph of Communism.

At which the 'simple country bumpkin' shook his head and pointed to the poster on the wall. 'Can't be done,' he said, this time in Hungarian, for the sake of variety. 'Not allowed.' Taken aback, the lieutenant-colonel read the notice published without his knowledge. It gave him quite a shock. Then he said to the man who had a gloating smile on his face, '. . . . .!!!!', got in his buggy, and drove away.

A decree ornamented with a big red five-pointed star was soon issued to the effect that the odious posters were to be removed immediately.

The 'simple country bumpkins' shrugged it off.

Who's got more pluck?

ÁVÓ officer Imre Macskási was renowned far and wide for his awesome strength. For instance, once he was standing guard in front of 60 Andrássy Road when he happened to think of a bit of mischief, and decided to sneak away for a fleeting hour or two, as his new brunette plaything held out the hope of exquisite delight. But delight here and delight there, he had to make sure that no harm would come to the house, so he grabbed an old millstone on Nov. 7th Square, dragged it back in his arms, and barred the gate with it.

But once he met his match in the shape of a Count that's seen better days. He took his car to be fixed, a sleek, steel-grey *Chaika*. When it was ready, Macskási said, 'Let me see that valve.'

'Here you are, sir!' the aristocratic progeny said rather too humbly. Since he couldn't get himself to say comrade and since he had nothing more to lose than what he had, he didn't even try. He lived the way he thought he should and as circumstances would allow.

'No good!' grumbled Macskáki in a *pseudo* manner, and snapped the valve in two, CRACK! as if it were a pretzel. The Count looked at him, his face a blank, and handed him another valve. He snapped that in two as well. The third, though, was all right. 'How much?'

'One unit,' says the Count. The comrade handed him the unit. 'No good,' said the other, and snapped it in two. He snapped the second unit in two as well. The third was all right, though. 'It'll do.' The surprised ÁVÓ officer gave his worthy opponent another unit as a reward for the good joke.

When the big steel-grey ark sped away, the Count sat down on the porch, leaned his head on his elbows, and stared into space. A cold shiver slithered down his spine. He ran his greasy fingers through his hair, then drew some strange signs into the dust. He did no more work for the day. His landlady puttered around him with concern. The next morning he got up at dawn, and so did Macskási.

Music

When the fomenting enthusiasm that was building – not to say *overrunning* – the country discharged itself once more in yet another spontaneous popular march, the company of merry men carried their banners down Andrássy Road. There was space aplenty, there was sunshine, there were girls and young women, their tresses flapping in the wind; there was freedom, there was energy unbounded.

At the entrance and corners of number 60, uniformed men with machine guns stood guard, while the sidewalk was made secure from the [*self-censored*] with heavy chains attached to quaint little posts. On top of the posts as well as on the windowsills of the front of the building, row upon row of red geraniums nodded their pretty heads at the machine guns. There was even music. Real music. The melody and rhythm to which we all danced was supplied by an ÁVÓ marching band. A man standing next to me started chuckling, his white head bobbing up and down from the force of his laughter.

'What's so funny, old man?' I asked, taken aback.

'Nothing much, son,' he said pointing to the enthusiastic, ruddy-cheeked musicians, 'except, I was thinking. When the time comes, how will these upright lads *prove* that all along they did nothing but *play*?'

The old man chuckled for some time yet. I had no idea that in him the purifying storm of the future was already brewing.

Cultural policy
'Révai could not forgive himself – nor me, for that matter – for liking my novel.'

'Honoured Colleague! if I construe your critical review aright, you are merely after my hide, but the book you seem to like. Thank you, dear friend, thank you!' (An ungenerous bosom pal.)

The misery of the small east-european nations

Then one fine day Miklós Horthy did an about-face and broke through his class-barriers. Humpty Dumpty sat on a wall, Humpty Dumpty had a great fall.

STOP

Once upon a time, the time being '49, the well-known humorist Pál Királyhegyi decided to come home. He took a good look around to see what there was to see, then went to the post office and sent the following telegram: J. V. STALIN MOSCOW THE KREMLIN STOP THE REGIME IS NOT ALL THAT IT'S SOUPED UP TO BE STOP KIRA-LYHEGYI STOP. That was it. Stop.

The artist's dream

Dream: L. (see *Revenge*, Part IV) and Pál Királyhegyi are strolling hand-in-hand down Vörösmarty Square, enjoying a good laugh at Stalin's expense. Tanks approach from Váci Street. *Tanxi!* waves Pál, and they cheerfully ride away.

For the Kodály year

Juicy cultural times, a reception. Mme Kodály, the maestro himself, plus Minister of Culture Révai. Mme Kodály to her husband with the severity of the partially deaf: 'Be careful, Zoltán! They say that man's a communist.' (True, this is only *half* the story. But that was the idea).

Mother is scared

('Your son is so *dashing*!') 'Oh, if only you could have seen him in the *olden* days, when in his bright, white cotton suit he rode out of a morning . . .' (Notices a matron, well endowed *from the left*, a Party lady, standing next to her) '. . . But oh, when I think of that old hag *under* him!'

Holiday

The Hotel Nádor, Pécs. A herald appears, wheezing, our beloved leader, he is dead, our blazing torch and lance, Stalin is dead. Horrific silence. The band stops. The waiters freeze in mid-motion. And little wonder. No one knows the etiquette for such occasions. And then, in this almost unbearable, dull, Asiatic (poor Pannonia! poor Hungary!) silence, someone (the uncle of a great poet, perchance?) gently taps the side of his teacup and in a low, pale voice says, WAITER, BRING THE CHAMPAGNE. He was released after n number of years (where $n = \geq 1$).

Esprit de corps

Two young people from the ÁVÓ tied the knot. The judge: 'Do you promise to love, honour and obey till death do you part?' And so it transpired. They loved, honoured and obeyed, but then death did them part.

The joke

'I have some good news and some bad news. The good news is that I have only *one* piece of bad news. And the bad news is that you, Comrade, are about to die.'

Flaubert at the ÁVÓ

'Miserable rat, do you still insist that *we were made to communicate and not to own each other*?!' (Flaubert: Corresp. II, quoted by Arnold Hauser in *The Social History of Art and Literature*). 'Well, then, here you are, lousy bastard, TAKE IT, IT'S ALL YOURS!'

Fragment

'Oh, don't, dear man, don't strike me, please!' – And she laughs from the heart.

Nostalgia: ÁVÓ disco

'Okay, everybody, now listen, for chrissakes, *time's money*, let's take it from the top again, from oh, don't, dear man, don't strike me, but laugh, damn it, laugh, don't grin, don't whine, I want no innuendoes, just laugh from the heart and make it authentic already, all right?'

Small business socialism

'Is it true that under socialism the streets are paved with gold?'

'Well, I wouldn't put it quite like *that*, Comrade, but you're gropin' in the right direction, Comrade, if you don't mind me saying so, Comrade.'

Creative writing practice

When he emerged from the tall, grim building where he had spent many long years, he squinted in the sunshine, almost staggered, but then did not; he turned back, the way we turn towards our paternal home as we set off on a long, unfamiliar journey. And there, on top of the building, glittered a red star. He withdrew *backwards*, thus staggering after all (the triumph of realism having snuck up on him), when the setting sun was gradually eclipsed by this sign, its contours shimmering as if they were the source of the radiance, the new holy sacrament of the new age.

'Exquisite,' he said in his heart of hearts with wry satisfaction, 'exquisite,' then sat down on the edge of the sidewalk. He sat for a long time staring into space, feeling the earth tremble beneath him as the great buses passed by.

It was early summer and the weather was unfolding. Had he raised his eyes he would have seen the women walk past in their light fluttering cotton dresses, and in the office across the street he could have spied the ladies as they perched on top of their desks, indolent and languid, crumpling the important official documents under their bums. They were just where they belonged, he would have thought.

But he saw only the fanciful eddy of dust on the asphalt, the bus tickets and cigarette butts stirring near his feet. Meanwhile it grew dark, and cool, too, quite precipitately. There was a change of guard in front of the building and one of the guards, a callow youth – the night had fallen by then – went over to the emaciated, pale stranger, put a hand on his shoulder, and said, 'Stand up, friend, you'll catch cold . . .'

And then, like a dense veil slowly falling from the starry sky, silence returned.

Love! Liberty![18]

Before I treat the decline of the age under scrutiny, I wish to
relate two frivolous stories I'd heard from my friend Lőrinc
Dániel.

The subject of the first will be liberty, the principal ideology of
the period. I do not care to mention the names, though I know
them, because it would cause hardship to the families, who are
flourishing again. The characters are the eternal characters, i.e.,
a *man* and a *woman*.

'Oh, Comrade, you are too cruel! Why do you reject my sensual,
passionate advances? Do not you see, my love, with your own
eyes, my love, how my bulging cock is rearing to be freed of the
prudish confinement of its breeches? Is not madam's lap as
willingly dewy as mine?'

'With mine eyes do I see the gigantic, boundless joy-stick which
is surely rearing for the wild, beastly leap, but thou art so . . .
unseemly!'

'For chrissakes, do you not know that we men are *at liberty* to be
a little on the homely side?'

'But you, my friend, do *abuse* said liberty . . .' _ _ _ _

The secondary story could perhaps be summarised under the
title, the ÁVÓ playing pussy-cat.

---

[18] In the fifties, a form of greeting, to which the common folk would respond, *'That's
all we need, plus the rain.'*

Two young ÁVÓ recruits, still as downy and fragile as a doe among the reeds and somewhat indolent by nature, decided to take a break, and so lay themselves down on the lap of the soft thick grass by the edge of a woodland meadow.

They lay on the grass for some time, their eyes probing the lilies of the field and the birds of the air; a bunting warbled, the moles were digging holes, the squirrels were chewing nuts, and the deer stuck their graceful heads out of the thicket only to steal away again. Further off a wild boar rattled the underbrush, while nearby the bough of the honey-locust bowed to the ground and the broom, too. After a while the boys turned around, clasping their hands behind their newly shaved, unprotected napes. Between their lips they were twirling some lovely daisies as lightly as if they were cigarettes. (The net-like imprint of the hardy grass would show on the back of their hands for some time yet, like someone whose hand went numb in sleep.) They watched the implacable march of the clouds and breathed deeply of the scent of spring and the scent of the good earth; among the blades of grass an army of ants went peaceably about their business as the yellow dandelions came jutting rudely into their sluggish field of vision.

All at once there appeared from the forest a pretty village lass gathering wild strawberries. And truth to tell, she had one helluva shaped, glorious whatnot. One of the two youths quickly leaped to his feet and barring the way, began to tease the frightened filly.

'Well, lass, you sure picked a choice spot. But you gotta pay a tariff, you know!'

'That's what you think,' said the woodland nymph who'd lost her way.

'It seems to me,' said the philosophical youth from the ÁVÓ, 'that if you'd pay for forbidden goods out of *necessity*, why wouldn't you pay *even more* willingly for goods that are not forbidden out of your own *free will*?'

'And how much would that be?' the little vixen asked with a faint blush.

'Don't you fret, *lambkin*, it won't be too high. Just an innocent little kiss.'

'So be it,' the little chit said, bravely squaring her shoulder. 'I can always spare a kiss for the people's republic. But don't think I'll bid *lower* than that!' And with that she quickly offered her lips to the startled ÁVÓ lad, then laughing merrily, took off. Like a fleeting melody, such is life.

Confessions of an eyewitness

We don't get to choose our parents, and we don't get to choose our friends. We do not love somebody because they are handsome or clever or of good character, not even because they happen to resemble us and thus, through this love, in a primitive and backhanded manner, into the bosom from behind, we end up raising our own esteem in our own eyes. No. We can love anybody.

I heard the story of the *decline* from my friend Lőrinc Dániel, who was one of its participants. Dániel lived in history, close to the forge. He is my friend, though I do not think I approve of all his actions.

We were sitting in the back room of the Folter Café. It had a less elegant aspect than the front room, more neglected, but also more exclusive and comfortable, its regulars more select. We settled at one of the dirty battered iron tables at the base of the fire-wall yellowed with water stains. I ordered beer, my friend two mugs of soda water (!). Margó, the thickset waitress, nodded, her face impassive, but when she put the mugs down in front of us, there was a touch of sarcasm in her gesture: *your water, sir*, she said exquisitely. Lőrinc Dániel caught none of this, and I loved him for it, even if at times it was rather embarrassing. He said nothing, just sipped his water. From time to time Margó shook past us. I had the impression that she *smelled of gasoline*. Lőrinc Dániel was as deeply silent as if his silence were definitive, all-encompassing.

Before he fell silent, though, he spoke about how morals had begun to decline among the people, how the distress they had faced had hardened them and, like sailors after weathering a storm, how they have become more wicked, ignorant and stupid in their reflections, more doggedly obstinate in their sins and immoral acts than they had been before.

'I, for one, would not go that far,' I said in my own cautious manner . . .

'I'd be hard put to say when it all started,' D. said as he launched into his narrative, 'how it began to stink, whether there was something you could point a finger at, something that came to life then died away, died away then came to life, or whether it was just that seeping through, the seeping through of fear which we recognise only after the fear has paralysed us and struck us mute. In short, I don't know how it *could* have started, and if so, when it took its start . . . And this weighs heavily upon me.'

(Albeit unintentionally, my friend L.D. had touched upon something vital. After all, people do not live in the Rákosi era or under King Mátyás's reign or in the whatnot of advanced socialism. Only the politicians talk like that in their arrogance, and also to scare us a little. 'Take it easy, fellow citizen, and thank God you are living in the era of the primitive accumulation of capital.' And we take the hint. But whether it unmakes us or elevates us to new heights, no, not like this; you simply can't turn an entire nation into a gaol house, because the bars are *someplace else*, because even if they shout until they turn blue in the face, we were young once, loud and self-confident, the world belonged to us because we loved and hated, betrayed and redeemed one another, then slowly we began to age, to fade, we cheated, pilfered, lied, made sacrifices, we eked out a living and scratched at the soil with all ten fingernails, we laughed and we held our peace. Our lives are shallow and magnificent. Compared to this Rákosi and his clique are small fry. Except . . . But let me give back the floor to whom it belongs.)

'Yes. But during our inquiry is it peace and quiet we are after, are we after happiness? No. Just the truth, be it ever so frightful and unsightly! . . . If it's peace of mind and happiness you're after, keep the faith. But if you want to be a pupil of truth, you must investigate! Between the two there are a dozen halfway points, but the primary goal is the primary goal.

'Time, too, passed in bits and pieces, somehow; it was and it was not (once upon a time there was, then there was not!); things happened of which we were ignorant, that's how we always put it in order to excuse ourselves as best we could, saying that these things happened *to us*; then after a while we noticed that these things *happened*, and so forth. I am not looking for excuses. *We were supporting actors in our own lives* at a time when everything blared forth the same thing: the time is here at last, and not only the factories are ours, but our lives as well. Instead of starring roles, however, we had to make do with a couple of *stars*. Thus did we side-step, more and more bitterly, into the future. In the meantime we lived and worked, of course. And were "building the country".

'One evening I reached home in a foul mood, beset by anxiety. I didn't know what to do. Everything was permeated by a big, bad, cavernous silence, for already people had, as it were by a general consent, taken up the custom of not going out of doors after sunset.

'Suddenly the door flew open and there stood my wife, Ilon Bagits, on the threshold, having just come back from her holiday that day. She was as radiant as a *Free People* magazine cover. But something was amiss. I could *feel* it.

' "What's got into you?" I asked softly. My voice was hoarse, *storyish, like my wife's*, short-tempered. I clung to the armrest of the easy chair, the blood draining from my hands. "What's got into you?" Ilon was still standing at the door with that aloof, dispassionate radiance I find so maddening. She smiled.

' "What? Nothing. Nothing's got into me. But I'm finding life a little peculiar," she added, her voice almost melodious. I couldn't take it any more and ran out to the street, breathing deeply in the velvety darkness. I stood around a bit in the spaciousness of November 7th Square, contemplating the cheerful, smiling faces of the nation's leaders.[19] Breathing deeply, I tried to divest myself of the dead weight settling on my chest.

'Just then I saw a crowd of people on Andrássy Road, all staring up into the air to see what a woman (?) told them appeared plain to her, which was an angel clothed in white, with a fiery sword in his hand, waving it or brandishing it over his head. She insisted it was Defence Minister Mihály Farkas. She described every part of the figure to the life, showed them the motion and the form, and the poor people came into it so eagerly, and with so much readiness: "Yes, I see it all plainly," says one; "there's the sword as plain as can be." And it was evening, I might add . . .

'I looked as earnestly as the rest, but perhaps not with so much willingness to be imposed upon; and I said, indeed, that I could see nothing but a white cloud, bright on one side from the light of the moon. At this the woman turned away from me, calling me a profane fellow, and a scoffer; told me that it was a time of God's anger, and dreadful judgements were approaching, and that despisers such as I should wander and perish.

'It was no use; I found there was no persuading them that I did not laugh at them, and that I should be rather mobbed by them than be able to undeceive them. Luckily something began to stir

[19] And oh, how they did smile upon us, *without end*, from banners and placards, bulletins and school-room walls, hospital rooms and dining-room walls. The obligatory etiquette: Lenin on the left, Stalin on the right, and our very own Rákosi stuck in the middle, his bald pate beaming into the distance.

at number 60 just then and a sleepy-eyed, good-looking youth equipped with a machine gun came outside very courteously requesting everyone, would they *kindly* go home to bed at this late hour, for tomorrow is another day, and though the enemy may not sleep, it was paramount that *they* stayed fit, *für alle Fälle* – just to be on the safe side. Since his line of reasoning was ever so cogent and delicate, the crowd soon dispersed.

'I was restless. All the excitement, it baffled me. All of it baffled me. The spell was nevertheless so convincing that I had to remind myself repeatedly of what actually *was*, and what this newfangled aesthetics boded. But the day was by no means at an end because on Jókai Square, where the auto shop is today, stood a man looking through the palisades where the [*self-censored*] lies today . . . In the full consciousness of my worth and in no uncertain terms I said to him, "It's really decent of you to be so concerned about my affairs. Frankly, I had no idea you had such a feeling for business."

' "Only other people's business." His eyes were bright as stars. Then right afterwards:

' "Now if you'll permit me, captain," he went on, "I will also make a note to myself." And he smiled at me shamelessly.

'This was the moment when I came to my senses. I shall never forget it. As surely as I am alive, he wrote down something about me.

'Oh, how many times I thought of that scene; how many nights I spent agonising over it. I would give a lot even today if I could put my hands on that notebook of his.

'Also, I had no idea what to do next.

'Because life, alas, depends on formalities.

'For instance, it would make no sense at all to start raging again, or act indignant, not after you've had a heart-to-heart with the fellow.

'Still, I wouldn't demure. I went up to him and, putting my hand under his chin, lifted his head, like a girl's, so he'd look in my eyes. He turned pale straight away.

' "Enjoy your notation, my friend," I said, meek as anything. And: "It's sure to be instructive," I added, meek as before. "And now, go!" I said abruptly.

' "Ah, you're throwing me *out*, captain?" And he even tried to laugh a little. He couldn't very well say much. I still had my hand on his chin.

' "Yes, I am," I said. "You gave me good advice, and I shall take it. But it is getting late." Meanwhile, my eyes were saying, I'll let you off this time. But if I get my hands on you again, you'll live to regret it.

'And with that we shook hands. Which was kind of funny. We even laughed over it, both of us. Even over this. Then he left.

'I stopped in the middle of the street and thought, so then. That's where we stand. I stood around for some time. And then I thought, it's all right. Whereas it wasn't. The minute I got home a puppy ran in front of me on the stairs. I tripped and tumbled down the steps.

'Several weeks before Rajk's arrest a blazing star or comet appeared in the sky. I saw the star myself and had so much of the common notion of such things in my head, of the variations of fear, that I must confess[20] I was apt to look upon it as the forerunner and warning of God's judgement, though I knew, too, that natural causes are assigned by the astronomers for such things, and that their motions and even their revolutions are calculated, or pretended to be calculated, and so it's unfounded . . . *unfounded.*

'My wife nursed me without a word of complaint. Once when I was convalescing and Ilon leaned over me to fix my damp, flat pillows and under her thin dress I saw her trembling and advancing boobs, like a schoolgirl's, maybe because she never had a baby, I'm afraid I propped myself up on my elbow and with one hand grabbed her neck and part of her cute little face; I pulled her down to me, but my illness had really weakened me, and so my elbow veritably caved in, which must have made the sequence of my movements appear stormy and terrifying. Ilon's head crashed into my groin.

'She couldn't control herself and screeched out in such a frightful manner, it was enough to fill the stoutest heart in the world with abject fear, nor did this *suffice*, but the fright having seized her spirits, she ran all over the house, up the stairs and down the

---

[20] *'I beg you. Anything. Just don't hit me. Please. Please.'*

stairs, like one distracted. This demented running on the stairs I could not allow, of course, because of the neighbours, for one.

' "What's the matter?" I asked after I had smacked her on the kisser. Ilon started hemming and hawing like when you're planning to tell a lie, then launched into some cock-and-bull story that was supposed to have happened to her, but in the story she referred to herself as some "gentlewoman", "an unfortunate lady of good breeding", and so on, like some stranger independent of her, and so for some time I had difficulty understanding what she was about.' [As the reader can see, my friend Dániel is doing likewise, to some extent. Married couples have much in common.] 'In short, *she* knows that *I* know how there's a shadow cast over us all these days while *some people* can walk around freely, and that one of these, one of these people was loitering on the corner of Váci Street and Kígyó Street, singing; the people said he was only drunk, but he himself said that he was a *free, independent, sexually mature male*, which later, near by today's Mézes Mackó buffet, he amended by saying that he was a dogmatic communist revisionist, in short, that he was ✤ and meeting the gentlewoman (!) she had just mentioned, he would kiss her, and so on, whereupon the unfortunate woman ran from him, but he, he took off after her and the like, calling her a "gentrified mare" and a "bourgeois bitch", and that in the end he did kiss her, and that's why Ilon was so terrified now.

'I didn't credit a word she said. She found me repulsive. We hated ourselves in the other. But sometimes there were no emotions involved. Once we went to the market on Lehel Square, looking for soup greens. A man was hawking tiny, colourful balloons. There was a sudden gust of wind and the balloons wanted to take off for the sky. Their owner tried to curb them.

' "Our dear, beloved mother," Ilon said, pointing. Just then a couple of balloons broke free and headed for the sky. Ilon was ecstatic.

' "*See? What must break free will break free!*" ' But this was just an episode.

'One mischief always introduces another. Terrors and apprehensions of the people led them into a thousand weak, foolish, and wicked things, which they wanted not a sort of people really wicked to encourage them to . . . Even the various institutions could not escape the general excitement. There were colleagues who repeatedly trespassed the bounds of moderation, trespasses that pain the soul just reflecting upon them. Honesty compels me to say this.

'Had the *object* of the mistake been only the old ruling class, well, for pity's sake, you gain some and you lose some, there's no war without casualties, our sympathies to the grieving family, easy come, easy go, such is life. The tragedy was that the working-class serpent bit its own tail . . . I dreamt I was two cats, playing a bloody game with each other. A bloody game. Then one morning, it was more like dawn, actually, they knocked at our door too and asked us to go with them. Towards evening they apologised and released us. (Back then we praised the day with the words, what a fine day we've had! Nobody's offered us their apologies.)

'They took from us our wallets, our watches, our fountain pens, our cigarettes, our lighters, our belts, our shoelaces. Sometimes at a run, sometimes feeling our way, tripping along the same room, deeper and deeper; it was always the same room. In the meanwhile the muteness was absolute, and so was the silence. The smell of oil and gasoline hit our nostrils in waves. The faces of the men looked more grave and terrified than excited. To the left were three small iron doors. The length of the room must have been about six feet, its width two and a half; the wall on the right was filled in with a board approximately a span and a half wide and fastened to an iron bracket. On this lay a horse blanket folded up multiple. The walls and the iron door, painted over with red lead, were covered with great drops of water which from time to time swelled into a stream of [*self-censored*]. A naked light bulb burned in a square-shaped recess.

'On the whole the face of things, I say, was much altered; no wonder the aspect of the city itself was frightful. Though I was convinced that the various strange events could happen only to others, the nagging doubt that maybe I was also ✤ took root. I was witness to most dismal scenes, as particularly of persons falling dead in the street, the terrible shrieks, and screechings of women, tried and true comrades, who in their agony would throw open their chamber windows and cry out in a dismal, surprising manner. It is scarce credible what dreadful cases happened in particular families every day. One was overcome by despair and madness, the other by incurable melancholy.

'Tears and lamentations were seen almost in every house, especially in the first part of [*self-censored*], for towards the latter end men's hearts were hardened, and death was so always before their eyes, that they did not so much concern themselves for the loss of their friends, expecting that they themselves should be summoned the next hour. I say it like it is. Perhaps it is a mistake, or was a mistake, but Stalintown, the new industrial showcase, did not sufficiently comfort me. The nation of steel and iron. Preposterous.'

This is the point where my friend Dániel fell silent in his own way; that is, he spoke a little about the decline of morals, that people had become more evil, stupid and reckless, and more doggedly obstinate in their sins since that time. After that we said nothing.

Then I turned to my friend Lőrinc Dániel and said: 'Many consciences were awakened, my friend, many hard hearts melted into tears; many penitent confession was made of crimes long concealed. Many a robbery, many a murder, has been confessed aloud, and nobody surviving to record the [*self-censored*].'

And Dániel answered me thus: 'What plenteous talk, what plenteous colourful, inflated soap bubbles, what jenny-wren flights under the wings of an eagle . . . And a people's republic for one wise word!' With a squeamish grimace he spilled a bit of water on the mud-packed floor. 'No one now dies of fatal truths. There are too many antidotes to them . . . People who give us their complete trust believe they have thus acquired a right to *ours*. This is a false conclusion; gifts procure no rights.'

And I said to my friend Dániel: 'We will be courageous, won't we, my dear, good friend? I have faith in one thing. That everything will be better, that *we ourselves* will be better, that we will grow in good intentions and good means to our ends, etc.' – Margó stopped at our table, listening in. Her breasts were like mountains. (*What're you staring at? It's all mine.*) – 'From now on our future is one, our faith is one, our hope is one! What you must go through I must go through, with neither of us being anything . . . anything good and true, by ourselves! Thank you, my friend, thank you.'

And Dániel answered thus: 'No. We must not talk about this, you and I. I will go even one step further. Two being as different as you and I cannot even keep silent about this together.' He took a sip of water. 'Where do we belong, you ask? We should be happy we can ask this question at all!'

And I said: 'Fathers have much to do to make amends for having sons.' I signalled to Margó that I wanted to pay. (*Your lips'll get chapped by the time you get to kiss 'em all around.*) Everyone has his price. This is not true. But there surely exists for everyone a bait he cannot help taking.'

And Dániel answered thus: 'One forgets one's sins when on has confessed them to another, but the *other* does not usually forget them.'

We got up. The beer stood in golden globules on Margó's unadorned tray. My friend and I agreed that when we'd meet we'd smile – and with good reason. Then I asked, 'What about Ilon?' 'No better than she should be,' he answered hastily.

But never mind. As Granny would say, 'Easy, boy, easy. Take it easy.'

III
('?')

*Of course there are then no questions
left, and this itself is the answer.*
(Wittgenstein)

What are we saying?

Take off your glasses? Come clean, sir? We know everything
anyhow? Don't shit in your pants, Kossuth?[21] Look, little
schmuck, we know the sun is shining and we know it is raining?
Come, come? Why this show of obstinacy?

The speaker uses the interrogative sentence to express his thirst
for knowledge and to call upon his listener to quench said
thirst? As a rule, the speaker's point of view is dubious in one
respect only? Generally, this is a lie? When we feel the necessity
of looking for a loophole in this manner, shouldn't we feel honour
bound to admit: we've got nothing left in stock? Which is
expressed by the most emphatic word in the interrogative
sentence?

---

[21] Lajos Kossuth: leader of the 1848–49 Hungarian freedom fights against the House
of Habsburg which, although they produced some impressive partial results, ended,
as always, etc., etc., etc.

All that beating about the bush, where did it get us?"[22] Where is Pálfi by now and what is he about? You crave rotten meat? With loving care for gravy? How is your worship's disposition for barren maidens tonight? Is the wolfman's power limited to a specific terrain, or is it universal?[23] How did distance beckon to Puss 'n Boots and take him away from us?

The riddle does not exist? If a question can be framed at all, it is also *possible* to answer it? For doubt can exist only where a question exists, a question only where an answer exists, and an answer only where something *can be said?*

I am in the *proper* place? I am here? I'm okay, I go for myself in a really big way? Are you open-hearted? A gentleman? Bellicose, proud, fearless and above-board? Brash, defiant, pleasure-seeking, apprehensive? Baleful? Obstinate, silent, withdrawn, a bit facetious, even? Is that why you lack trust? Are independence and autonomy your greatest treasures? Are you a freedom-loving Kurucz?

At the foot of the tall, luxuriant pines the bit of quivering snow appears ludicrous, the faded forest litter jotting through, while on the branches of the scant thicket the flakes of snow tremble like a fancy net that's seen better days? In the gardens the tenacious bindweed creeps up the birch trunks while haphazard spaces open up to make room for the piercing rays of the sun among the boughs?

The backs of our scawny hags are steaming?

---

[22] Oh, all that indolent beating about the bush, it got us nowhere.
[23] A difficult question to answer (given the present state of things).

But if one or another of our capricious clouds-in-the-sky so enjoins, a dull drabness descends swiftly on the land, greyness coming upon greyness; only very high up in the firmament does a hint of colour appear, a blemished shade of red, giving the land an even more sordid aspect?

Tortured, tormented, like a weeping eye? The traditional Magyar costumes, see them dangle from the branches of the big, leafy trees, an elaborately trimmed cloak, a short *mente* lined with fox fur, a kerchief wrought with spun gold, a wide pleated skirt and a cherry-coloured hussar's pelisse, of velvet? The grey slush settles on the soft leather boots? *Do you approve of this?* Conversely, do you disapprove? You couldn't care less? Not a fig? Or you know not what to think? You have never experienced great difficulties, you have never been made to run the gauntlet? Well? The memory of a childhood humiliation, at least?

A helpless *shifting in place?* A creaking parquet floor? Mayonnaise potatoes slithering around your plate? Have you been made to eat humble pie? How many? Or have they broken off your horns? Been cut down to size? Life's thrown you *a bad curve?* In grammar school? In high school?

Once, for instance, you had to bring the skeleton of a frog to biology class, *quasi* as your reward? A mistake, having joined that stupid study circle? You should've had more pluck? No use crying over spilled milk? Wandering aimlessly by the Danube between the Árpád Bridge, named after the first Magyar chieftain, and that other, christened after Liberty, the one outcome of which was that you became the *terror of the fishermen*, which ain't nothin'? In the end it hit you and you drove out to City Park lake? Cussing your pretty biology teacher in no uncertain terms, you strolled along the stone footbridge while in the distance two girls giggled in a boat? One of them was Drahosch?

Leaning over the side, you rubbed your groin against the balustrade hard as you could and for as long as you could? Working in minuscule, invisible circles, you clenched your teeth while your poor little heart went pit-a-pat? Frightened like a doe, you glanced around but could see nothing suspicious? *A stone groin?* Well worth it, shame notwithstanding? *As a general rule do you suppress or sublimate?* Work *through* it? Work it *in*? Artistic form? Or ethical bedrock? Are you plotting, scheming, conspiring, double-dealing *amiably*? Setting traps in the old manner? Stab in the back, abort and torpedo? Are you some sort of vermin? A rat? Or the transition that eases remembering?

What did you do the first time it hit you? You were nineteen and you were sitting for all you were worth on the school john and when you got home you tried not to look anyone in the eye?

Are you passionate?
Kurucz and passion, Kurucz and manly verve are as inseparable as the Bobsy twins? Are you in favour of manly verve *without democracy*? Have you ever had a real democratic experience to begin with? Do you think it is important that you should?

Do you have (have had, could have) such an experience under the following conditions: self-delusion – bloody battles – nationalistic sentiments (a little manual democracy) – grammar?

What are the symptoms? What position are your legs in?

Does it give you a thrill? Have you, jocularly speaking, laid an egg and liked it? You wouldn't give it up for a bushel of gold? You're as pleased with it as a fool is with his own shadow or a blind man with a wooden penny? Or is it six in the morning and half a dozen at night? Perish the thought?

Even the scum are delighted?

Never say die? Or is that going too far? How far? Everything leading to the dictatorship of the proletariat is heavenly, divine? Of course, the end does not justify the means? (Who knows why, but some go in for full openness and abandon, while others opt for constraint, dogmatism, it being their hobby-horse? Still others fall to their knees and raise their voices in supplication while, conversely, certain people, their feet beating about in the air, wheeze with every breath as if they were playfully practising standing on their heads?)

First impressions can be decisive? The times? '49, '67, '19, '45, '56, '68? Do you play the lottery, madame? There is always a number, *rational*, *positive*, even *whole*, which is surrounded by either silence or fanfare whereas it should be reflection, deliberation and ethics? And the like? To be a democrat means first and foremost not to be afraid?

Let us speak for once the way the Lord would have us?
The time is not ripe, friends?

Who're you calling friend, friend? Oh, don't, sweetie pie, you mustn't? As we straddle the borderline of our knowledge and opportunities, mum's the word? Let us predicate the way we are used to? I'm okay, you're okay, he goes for himself in a really big way? We should make bold? Clear out of the way, lose our edge, lose interest, denounce, take to wing, wander about aimlessly, die of mortal fear? Settle for the common denominator? Impose burdens, fume with rage, shy away, dance the shilly-shally, hold out to the last breath, be wary and circumspect? Or *guardedly* credulous?

Let's synchronise our intentions?

Nurse a yellow streak, go for it, worm our way, side-stepping, flake off, get the hell out? Slavering and drivelling at the mouth? Full peace-environment, peace supplies? You betcha? We should stammer and stutter, act deplorably, colour our efforts individually, be *demi-mondain*, go for the fun? Oh, ye crowds of rags and patches, frail, sinful and beggarly, what about it? I hate you, my homeland, may a fly walk across your open eyes?

What's going on here?

Where here? Let us make a fuss, be base, not worth our weight in salt? You are content? Oh, young sir, how refined, the way your cute little heart doth pound pound pound? Or will this a discreet shading yet receive? The Kurucz craves understanding? There's such a whole lot we could give one another?

In short, we're easy as pie? A song stands ready to burst trippingly from the tongue? THE WATCHWORD: INGRATIATE? Democracy is rebirth, the awakening of life, springtime, pleasure, radiant, exciting, exquisite, outta sight? The ideal way to relax after a hard day's day? Who're you kidding?

In your joy you wag your own tail? Wiggle your ass? Or eager and explosive, generally grab yourself a woman on the run? What do you think: does the dictatorship of the proletariat *happen* to you, so to speak, or, conversely, are you making *it* happen? The woman does not speak, nor does she move, she merely grabs the corner of the hearth, lowering her eyes like one who does not mind what is going on behind her in the night? She imagines what she hankers for? An old hag enters to put more wood on the fire? When she sees the two of you, her face breaks into a devilish grimace, but you don't mind her presence in the least, and grinning she cackles, *ride her, your excellency, ride my good, kind mistress?* The woman straightens up and, sighing, fatigued, shaking at the knees, her innards battered, a moist, wet smile playing on her lips, she lowers her big round eyes and stumbles out?

The second shall be Clara of the eloquent behind, grab her boobs, see if she minds? Her beaver scrapes the Kurucz's belly?

I prefer to be wearing tight blue jeans, sometimes I apply baby oil to my tits and belly, and I don't mind telling you what it feels like when I unscrew the head of the shower hose – a rose is a rose is a rose – a gallant Kurucz am I? (*Wow!!! what a question, even with my panties on* ...) Timid and anxiety-ridden, easy-going and blindly trusting, morose and spiteful, my intellect subdivided, working in large units, even-keeled, simple, compact? I can heave a donkey off the ground by the tail? I can take care of myself, I keep in tune with my self and my body, I am *here*, I'm okay, I go for myself in a really big way? We declare war on lies, hypocrisy, dullness and cowardice? We are shooting at random, not so much at given targets, but rather to impress the populace we've jolted out of its slumber? To disturb the peace?

It is time somebody tied a knot on this endless string of thread?
Sons-of-bitches-of-the-soul?

Embedded in cultural history, the balls nailed down?

Trust to time to find a way? From the walls of the former besieged
castles (*ex*: Brasov), unflagging and obstinate, the rain continues
to wash away the traces, the centuries dull the high brilliance of
the towers, the firmament like a piece of pergamon crowded with
writing a long, long time ago, at the bottom the seal crumbling
like the disc of the sun going down in a storm before anyone
could have supposed that at dawn the fog would lift from the
funereal plains, the flax open its blue flowers, and the dew wash
clean the berries glistening from their poisonous deadly night-
shade? It is cold, says Miska Halassi, then turns away from the
window? The wind creeps through the thick walls?

My lips chapped, I stand in front of the large oval tray, of silver,
hung on the wall in place of a mirror? It hardly distorts at all,
my face dignified and pale, *beaten silver*, as night descends? Outside the black trees disappear, the hard-packed snow gleams icy-
white, the loathsome Labancz lurk on the edge of the woods,
sweet German lords adorned with ribands, raven-black grena-
diers, cavaliers, lean-flanked dogs, hairy-legged canines with ribs
of woven twigs, the moonlight gleaming on their eye-teeth, the
melancholy woven of this light, the wild pack of moon-coloured
dogs? I smooth my hand over the indelible grooves on my forehead, an uncertain fire crackling in the hearth, what ignominious,
abject poverty! – am I hoping to sail away on a sea of bliss?

Will you kindly provide a couple of *sketches* of situations in which
you saw a chance, however slight, for the dictatorship of the

proletariat? In these uncertain times you can see by anybody, and try, too, what's in people's hearts, who you should bend a knee to, or bow your head?

Are they teasing your sense of justice? How? Hypothetically speaking, for the sake of argument? Does this particular form of manly verve mean a lot to you? How much of a lot? They're teasing your linguistic sense too? D'ya dig it daddy-o like, so much fiddle-faddle, or enraged and terrified, your life's blood is drained from you?

How do you achieve the delicate balance of your sense of justice? Lengthy shilly-shallying, indirect teasing? Is an alert conscience of the essence, or just a matter of custom? What's yours like? Groggy? It even snores? And now a word or two about lullabies? Well? The projection of colourful wish-fulfilment images on the water-stained wall of the imagination? Or in the wake of a substantial surprise attack from the flanks, holding the poor somnolent city to ransom, do you prefer to reduce its stone walls to rubble and carry off the city elders?

If in the midst of a bloody battle a democratic experience should happen to advance on the scene, what do you prefer, the politics of the hard fist – the soft – the fast – the slow? Complete or partial penetration into problems, penetration, then holding still? Do you give primacy to a thought's greatness and shape? Which in your opinion is *most fortunate*: the long and traditional, the short and traditional, the thin but resourceful, and so on?

Or lying low and holding your breath? Waiting breathlessly for that breathless moment? At which juncture you unwittingly play with the bonds of social responsibility? I should have it so good?

Do you like to do it from the back? Are you often asked to? In what manner? Who asks you? Does the little devil with the horns and hoofs appear from the murky corners of nondescript bus stations? Or do you happen to be sitting with your beautiful sweetheart at a table spread with a yellow cloth, a candle burning with a sputter because the wick is long, an accordion player seated nearby and a single man on the drums, as in the manner of two old maids you discuss the weather, the soccer scores and the difficulty of making ends meet – when one of the waiters describes a big circle with a hazel switch? Whereupon the food turns saltless in the blinking of an eye, the women can't conceive even amidst pain, all becoming fertile, all of them, and the candles stink? But it mustn't phaze you, the two of you should just look on? The waiters wink encouragingly, the accordion player, jocularly speaking, takes over, circling dreamily among the tables, sprinkling white powder from his filthy pocket, in all probability salt? To quiet her we grasp our beautiful sweetheart's trembling alabaster hands? The vodka glasses depleted, the marrow desiccated in the bone, vermin in the potato croquettes, the griddle-cakes crumbling, pink worms in the meat, the liver dumplings dry as stone?

The accordion player throws outdated slang around, real cool, the single drummer is real cool, an awkward virtuoso, while at your table the waiter bows confidently and begs your pardon for the slight *malheur*? The accordion player breaks into the national anthem for all he's worth, with possibly even a false note slipping in now and then, and with an obsequious smile the waiter asks whether your sweetheart mightn't be *needing* something *more*, whereupon you spring to your feet and with conviction though awkwardly slap the waiter's face? Then they beat the shit out of you?

Are other forms of manly verve and passion (social work, tree planting, aiding the underprivileged, the peace movement, retirement, etc.) important to you? Or would you rather, *sans gene*, be a party to a bit of irredentist nationalism? Onward to the breach, dear friends?

Are you a regular? Since when? Those droll years again, in ascending order? Does this affect your passions in any way? Have you any experience being *irregular*? Have you dipped the cold steel in anyone's bosom yet? What was it like? Did it affect your relationship, and if so, in what manner? How 'bout the trade union? Are you a materialist, or do you prefer to turn in supplication to the god of the Magyars while you brazenly blaspheme against the Virgin Mary herself? Conversely, would you rather keep all eventualities in mind? If you are a lone wolf, to what extent does this depend on choice? Have you any idea who is whose wolf? Who is whose what?[24]

Are you in favour of internecine war? Hungarian scratching out the eye of Hungarian? Of course, who *is* Hungarian? All enemies – yours – are *ab ovo* homeless villains? Are you of Hungarian mother born? Did you suck milk that was *likewise*? You, if they ask you nice, will give the shirt off your back (by the way, are you familiar with Hungarian sayings?), but not your wild oats? You're of two minds? Is the second of any use? Any use at all? You cry, laughing into your beer? A stranger to fear and trembling? With no need of a pardon? How about an interpreter? You

---

[24] If the text is from the thirties of the 20th century, then this is an oblique thrust at Admiral Horthy (who headed the country's semi-bourgeois, semi-democratic government), but in a way so that his fascistoid prime minister Gömbös should also get the message. If not, not.

carry your heart on the tip of your tongue? It is easy to seat you on a high horse but hard to get you off? Might you be wearing blinders?

If for some reason and regardless of the price (!?) you are opposed to slaughter because a severed arm, even if bourgeois, makes you retch and the sight of a man's guts hanging out of his belly neither fills you with joy, nor can you see any benefit in it – in short, if you are a squeamish humanitarian – what do you think of this state of suspended animation? Would you recommend it to others? What are your plans? How much longer?

The defiant troops come sweeping down the gulf, the stirrups working overtime, the hoofs thundering, the gentle valley reigning over the peaks; a bullet whizzes past with noble death for its passenger – but you just stand around, feeling desperate at best? You think we should crack down on this sort of national passion? When? In early childhood? Grammar school? High school? Or if not, why? It already is?

What does a Labancz smell like?

What is your opinion of revolution?
Do you feel, along with me, how pleasant it is talking about these things, how pleasurable the way we share a common understanding? Is the freedom-loving Kurucz attracted to another freedom-loving Kurucz or to a subjugating Labancz? Or, given that he is a Kurucz, it's six of one and half a dozen of the other? A step towards self-realisation? *Or something entirely different?* The cat's whiskers?

And another thing?

May God grant us peace –

We have played foul with our souls? They would have us do the lord's work? (*À propos*, are you a progeny?) Necessity is a great lord, but impossibility is greater still? We have swallowed the bitter pill? Or the frog, as they say? Out of necessity, not out of choice? In any case, the lake at City Park proved to be an area rich in frogs? Right away you started walking across the little footbridge with not a care in the world, trying to recall the problem of the bridges of Königsberg, because you were also in the maths study circle? A *musterkind*? Leaning over the water, you pressed your groin against the balustrade which was exactly the right height, and working in minuscule circles invisible to the naked eye you wriggled, writhed, twisted, thrust and humped rhythmically? Or was it more like a light touch? Your little heart racing? In the distance, two girls giggled in a boat, goodness is its own reward?

One is fair, the other oafish and fickle, gorges herself, her growth stunted, a blabber-mouth, her lower thighs ungainly and her posture crooked, her body thick, her figure ungainly and her teeth ungainly, her lips dark and shapeless, her face awry, her eyes myopic and her hair too thin, her smell unpleasant, her discharge too liberal, her breasts lumbersome and pendulous, she likes singing and instrumental music, ecstasy when it is complete, her lips like sails, her nose flat, she herself dwarfish and humpbacked, a black line running between her breasts, she's covered all over with pimples, disgusting, not too hot and not too cold, her thick, coarse beaver scars the Kurucz's belly, she's in love and due to the smell of her concupiscence it is impossible to stay anywhere near her, her walk is like an elephant's in heat, her breasts bawdy and lascivious? She is truly ugly?

No two ways about it?
It was the same girl you saw later on, towards evening on the suburban train heading home? Despite the black line running between her breasts, one look and you clapped her to your bosom? Conversely, you were ticked off, hating her superficially because she made you realise how alone you were, all by yourself?

Despite your tender years, you are *an expert on solitude?* An old fox in this sphere who'd seen more things in heaven and earth? Horatio? You were a frequent night traveller on the local and all too familiar with that desperate procrastination with which you tried to manipulate time? To make it stop? To make it turn around? Be something *different?* But the City Transport Authority is as reliable as death? What you really need is a woman? The light of the many-branched candelabra falters, the *Kappelmeister* waves to his small band, little vermin, the silks swish past again, the stockings fall lazily around the calves, our hot breath quickens, our face covered with crimson, and we sweat inside our light, chequered coat, our tie flying like a willow in the wind, the dust settles on our crimson boot, we try to guide our susceptible *cousines* towards the Magic Box and when, pretending chastity they carefully open it, they leap back with a scream, but their eyes sparkle with triumph?

In the dewy hours of the early morning you tried, really tried, rushing about your business, to read from the sleepy eyes of the women the story of their nights? How and in what manner they had passed? Searching, you looked for bags under their eyes, those tattle-tales of idyllic hours, the *sweet* saliva in the corners of their sulking lips? Where oh where are those *telling* traces? And since we're on the topic of trains, might we say that you'd go out of your way for a glimpse of those bags of idyllic hours? Your ideas were murky at best, but the murk was pleasantly warm, isn't that right?

The distinct silhouette of an aunt of sorts, a distant relative from Prague, comes leaping to the mind's eye, especially the pleated silk skirt as it came tumbling, so to speak, from her full hips giving the impression of an *exclusive* Young Pioneers skirt, which probably served to calm her conscience (*re.* the difference in our ages and our being related), anyway, during a seashore holiday in a distant place – and this can be ascertained after the fact – wanted to *make* you *love* her, but being *inexperienced*, you simply did not *catch on*, for which later, on many a lonesome Saturday, you'd have liked to bang your head against the wall? Or wherever?

In those days you were repeatedly irked by the way the woman was acting, not understanding, for instance, why being an adult she should giggle so much, why she leaned so close to your cute little cheeks for no reason at all (the smell of tobacco!), or why she made such snide remarks about the willowy daughter of the hotelier, the same age as you, why, when with your spirit in the dumps you complained that the lass refused to play *dodge'em* at the nearby amusement park, the woman called her a puny little toad, an insipid milquetoast, even a sly you-know-what, trying to ease your way to maturity, of which she could have used some herself?

What you so squeamishly resented, this lack of sobriety – the woman was obviously uneasy, though not overmuch, you weren't that important – you saw and suffered from it being so out of proportion? The high and low point locked in a stranglehold? You were standing on the shore attentively watching some ball game when the woman ran up to you with her by now habitual, overeager laughter and playfully covered your eyes with her hands from behind while you, just as habitually, *knew it all* instantly, who and what, rudely tossing her hands from you, but this rudeness did not dampen the woman's spirit, conversely, she provoked you openly and gleefully inasmuch as she made the overloud announcement that in a game of catch you, let us face it, are no match for her, whereupon with a blatantly cocky gesture that you had inherited or learned from your father you measured the woman from head to toe, then took off without further ado, the greedy watching of the ball game having whetted your appetite for action, you broke gingerly into a run along the long, gentle curve of the shoreline, bounding on the borderline of earth and sea, enjoying the pungent smell of the ocean and the splashing of your feet in the sand, then into the shallow water, unselfconscious as a puppy, sprinting, making sand and water fly, sometimes slowing down, at others leaving the woman to fend for herself, then as you let her catch up, you saw the purple rouge on her lips and the bubbles of red saliva in the corners, at the time you thought this disgusting and were about to pick up your pace again, but then the woman shouted, *wait, I can't keep up*, and like a *grand seigneur* you let her catch up with you; the woman was still laughing, laughing and wheezing as she unselfconsciously flailed her arms about in the water, which you regarded with detachment, from a high horse, as it were, then the woman sprang at you, screaming *gotcha*, calmly, you stepped back, thumbing your nose at her brand of mischief, the underhand and inexpert attack, it could have been easily averted, but you, God only knows why, would not budge, conversely, the touch of the woman's raised arms, so unexpected, and the simultaneous glimpse of the dark of her armpit frightened you and with a too sudden, panic-stricken movement you fell back, and before you knew it, you were wrestling in spite of your will in the outrageous mud puddles left behind by the tide, laughing, the woman churned up the water with her arms, it was dense with sharp grains of sand, desperate, you tried to peel her off, being pretty nearly smothered to death, your face pressed against her body, you couldn't be blamed, certainly, you were desperately thinking of a wrestling grip *that would not be against the rules*, but all this happened much slower than when you wrestled in school, and when with a cunning, relentless leg-lock (which worked *wonders* the other day against Korom) that wound around the woman's thighs, diminishing her pleasure in the pretended attack and replacing the laughter with a sort of anxious high spirits and sense of expectation, you, having attained a suitable position, heaved yourself up and away from her, *what? are you nuts?* you screamed familiarly, since you were related, which though not an essential, was yet sufficient cause (maths study circle!) of the familiarity, the woman turned away, lying on her back, furious, you sat with your legs crossed under you, the woman's hair was wet from the wet sand, which you thought was repugnant and *unbecoming*, abruptly, the woman got to her feet, ran her hands down her sides and waded into the water, by which time you were in a state of nervous excitement, then your backside started shivering, you stood up, your whole body covered with goose-bumps, treading slowly, your relative emerged from the sea, *let's go home*, she said softly, and since she did not look at you, you looked away, too, you didn't feel cold any more, you walked by her side with lithe steps, then you offered her your hand without a word, hers was cold, yours hot, and you walked on like that, hand in hand?

Once you saw her in the shower, caught a glimpse, probably by accident, thought the woman's hand might possibly have been in it as a conscious element? The water was running down her skin, her body, covered with the pearly drops of water, bending this way and that, she closed the door slowly, without haste, with an artlessness that would have charmed anyone else, but shocked you a little, *timidly shocked you*? You *imbibed* the unexpected gift of the naked body? The woman wagged a saddish, nicotine-stained finger? If you close your eyes now, the tawdry red of the fingernails still flashes at you, trance-like? Then later, as a grown-up, when you no longer suffered for want of women, you thanked heaven? A Pharisaic but excusable thought?

Which reminds me? In what manner do you pull the wool over your own eyes? Do you ever catch yourself doing it? Have you ever seen anyone else do it? Once you saw someone wet a middle finger? You are all for theoretical constructions, the unstable systems indigenous to our part of the world in which even the slightest change in the initial conditions, things, facts and truths will produce powerful changes?

Or how about a stupendously clever sentence that'll turn the world upside down *inconspicuously*? Well? Or a sentimental crusade, perhaps, against yourself in the course of which you are quickly overcome by yourself, finding yourself lovable, worthy and honourable, and so you end up taking the bait anyhow? Dangling the proverbial carrot in front of your own nose? You resort to linguistic terror? Or go in for similes and sayings? Calling the lips of the common folk to your aid? The literary classics? Politics? Religion? Ma(r)xims? Or do you use your finger (my pet), your hand, your palm? A beer bottle, a sheet? The border of a coverlet? Your teddy bear?

Though who is to say what we feel leaning forward on the backs of our horses, the warm, steamy animals, and what sitting down, sitting in the dark, on a damp stone, while the fog seeps in and out of our skull and the distant wind brings snatches of hurrahs that sound like sighs?

In order to satisfy our sense of justice we take two or three concrete facts into account? *Feed the old bitch?* The rest, the left-over facts, we use to cover up the ethical anomaly? THE WATCHWORD: GOD HELPS THOSE WHO HELP THEMSELVES? A question of pride and inhibition, I guess?

One of my nipples is larger and more sensitive? From time to time I nip, pinch, twiddle, tweak, and twaddle it? Our mother wrings her hands?

In the delirious, tense moment before it hits us we are broad-minded, liberal and progressive, I raise my bum and whip the horses, they pull back their little ears, *giddy 'ap?*, while, with slow, circumspect movement of the muscles the boys wipe patriotism right off the menu?

Everything's got its own story?
When the democratic experience takes its start we gotta expect a bit of *movement*? The desertion of pluck? It's like we've been wounded, no wonder if we're just a *bit* alarmed? But once we get the hang of it, self-delusion is like a great liberating ventilator, our mane majestically flapping in the wind, while at long last we can keep our passions in check, so that before long the feeling of pride should blossom forth, the pride of the Kurucz who was thus able to surprise *himself* with a first-rate present?

We rarely consider that being a freedom-loving Kurucz is not only a masterpiece of logic in face of the subjugating Labancz but also a colourful and highly complex theoretical construct in its own right? The ease with which the freedom-loving Kurucz play-at democracy[25] as part of their self-delusion would seem to contradict the popular cliché that the needs of the Kurucz in this sphere are innocent, childishly whimsical, and that the Kurucz would accompany a real despot to the ends of the earth? The Kurucz cannot leave himself out of account, i.e., his duty and his right to take stock of what is around him?

We face the danger of going about our new business too well? After all, we may find passion for its own sake, when subject and object, thief and gendarme, active and passive, starting point and ending point, cause and effect are identical more to our liking than our honoured imperial adversary whom we are startling out of his secure quarters, perhaps at the first break of a chilly dawn; like a dolt does the poor bastard sit on the edge of the comfortable peasant bed, the sulphurous fumes of the night shooting up from the enormous yet feather-light eiderdown that's shooting up from the bed, yellow clumps hang in the corners of his eyes, the back of his head is all abuzz as if a thousand playful devils had taken up their habitation there, he slips his cold, clammy feet into his damp boots, his foul clothes are limp and revolting, like a snake's cast-off skin, on the brick kitchen floor the *goodwife* stands wringing her hands on her long chemise and dipping one

---

[25] Sometimes we use this expression, *to play at democracy.* It is a verbal phrase. The active form of the verb is intended to modify the popular notion which compares the dictatorship of the proletariat to that biblical heavenly manna, as well as the idea that it appeared, fully armed, like Athena from the forehead of Zeus; it is further bent on shedding light on the possibilities open to the Kurucz, and in the final analysis denies the possibility of innocence.

thick foot in the lukewarm cinders, her dark groin showing through the thin white cloth as if a shade had settled there, a strange, mute animals, her two industrious hands held pressed to the bottom of her belly, our imperial adversary is making great haste, *sapperlot!* he cries, a plague on all their houses!, wheezing angrily as he fumbles with his boots, he dashes across the kitchen without so much as a sideways glance at the woman, he is right to make haste, our naked irons are waiting for him outside?

Improbable as it may seem, the sons of the nation feel no great inclination to look for symptoms of self-delusion? Whereas? Whereas it should be a holy rite? Indubitably? Because it depends on *us*, *we* keep it in check, it gives *us* false hope? A small step in the direction of freedom nonetheless? Because it is still preferable that we should *do ourselves in* than that we should have to stare into the smug countenance of some sweaty, mangy, shock-headed German scrambling after us like a bitch in heat, his face afire, while every part of our body hurts like the dickens?

It hurts

To prevent our sense of justice from getting inflamed, we have recourse to a number of fabulous *creams*? A pocket torch shining between our thighs? The warmth oh how good it feels?

Outside the damp night, a ruinous draught circling in the region, we paste our hand to the crevices, a sharp draught sucks at our palm, the intimation of remote peaks, long, deep valleys, everything grey, blue and brown, gentle and austere? Elegant and barbaric? I bolt the doors and lie motionless, hardly breathing, staring into space? I am repulsed by myself, I am clammy, I am alone, it is cold? The wind whistles through my ribs, the wind

whistles through my cheeks, snow sticks to my eyes, snow sticks
to my forehead, my throat is bare, my throat is bare?

Courageous, despairing, devil-may-care, family-loving, sombre,
amicable, cocky, congenial, tenacious, windy, dark, gay, wise,
cantankerous, despondent, reckless, cautious, curious, loyal,
fickle, proud, self-mocking, a living, breathing individual, ever
changing human beings: that's what we are?

You don't say?
We tailor ourselves to suit the times? Trying to make the best of
it in a nest of magpies? We know which way the wind blows? First
we please, then we fleece? Have we lost our better judgement? Or
are we clever operators? Taking the bait we got hooked in the
weir? The world has thrown us over its shoulder? *Say sibon?*

On the highway of our reflections we have reached the milestone
infested with idle, *lurking* dogs, at which point we accept that
the freedom-loving Kurucz has the right, imagistically speaking,
to himself – just a long as the Kurucz remains a Kurucz, i.e., he
accepts the subjugating Labancz, thereby legitimising the noble
hatred he feels, the communal games in blood and mire?

Or will the day come when we need no longer engage in battle
with the shield-bearers of prejudice but will take our pleasure
in living, living our drab and fantastic lives, discovering and
familiarising ourselves with ourselves (self-realisation!), and not
only in the confines of our narrow rooms will we feel the prompt-
ing to do this, or in a stinking, damp cellar with rotting straw,
or hiding in the dark depths of a forest, but together, out in the

open, with other 'individuals', the Kurucz, the Labancz, together,
we Hungarians?

**Something is rotten in the state of? It can't be so good it ain't bad?
We're a bunch of doubting Thomases?**

Anything might happen? Gotta expect a bit of scramming?
Scramming, scooting and skedaddling? The desertion of pluck?
Or it hitting you? We pull our beautiful butterfly blanket over
our head, our body floating in space, alive, throbbing, bursting
into bloom, hurting as we enjoy, our head light and reckless, the
noises remote as if we were hearing the sound of a horn from
the far-off Alps, time trickles slow as molasses, the space fragile,
everything pleasurably hot, warm, throbbing, dark, everything
searing hot, scorching, fucking good – *in the best sense of the word*,
the body fluid and soft, I can't move, my body knows no limits
there, I can't say this is good, this is not, I make no value
judgements, I accept, I am this act of acceptance, existence
without a backbone, assuming that objects have ethics: that's it?

Oooh! Democracy on the back seat of a Pobyeda —

We should take this fucking time more seriously?

Let's not despair? We're looking for a needle in a haystack? Or
just a subjugating Labancz with a heart of gold? Chasing our
own illusions, may God help us? I go about my business, except
that in the meantime I look ludicrous in my own eyes? Our
imperial adversary breathing down our neck, his knobbly knee
jabbing into our thigh?

Not only the mangy imperialist Labancz but the informed public too expects the freedom-loving Kurucz to be passionate, so fuck it? Better be nothing than mediocre? Moth-eaten? I'm thinking here of the bungling fools and the Labancz-chauvinist-pigs? But cause and effect are as jumbled up as the cards in the hand of a bad player? We're not playing at democracy, so who cares? Oy, oy? Haven't we turned into a 'Labancz service' of sorts already? – But a pox on it, if I give their rotten, blighted, cankerous kind a bit of false hope, don't I deserve a little something in return? For him to wait a bit, at least, till the shit is beaten proper out of him?

I want to be the hero of my own life. We are standing, standing in place, with anticipation watching our agitated, unkempt adversary who, with the stolen chickens under his arms, is scramming through the deep mud of the yard, the loathsome coat of the imperialists stretching across his bent back, his face red, dear man, he hasn't eaten in weeks either, our searching fingers could feel along his sweet, skeletal frame with compassion, his hips as they stick out, his ribcage as it sticks out, his collarbone as it sticks out, his shoulderblade as it sticks out, the vertebrae of his spine as they stick out in a row, the shoulders as they droop down in a curve, the prickly, lonesome nape with its pus-marked pimples, the dry, wrinkled, parchment-yellow skin, the deep scratch-marks (vitamin deficiency!), the poor, gnarled elbows, and the abused hairs on his chest? The straw on the sleeve of the threadbare coat is covered with shit?

What a scene, watching from our *place of hiding*, seeing the worked-up farmer run for the pitchfork, livid, from whence such determination? such reckless daring? such courage? such brashness? oh from whence, when for soothe no Chaunteclere doth flutter its wings any more, the watchdogs lambent, the cows tearful at death's door, and the young lamb bleating, trembling? from whence, when the stallion has been freed of its tether, but not us, it can't stand up, it just raises its sunken, bright, purple eyes upon its beloved master, the fire-kitten is purring atop the wooden roof, no woman sobs, speechless, she just clutches her bloody petticoat – and from our good vantage point we can even observe the shabby fellow lying in wait at the gate covered with black tar as he is about to raise his gun to his shoulder?

This waiting, always this waiting? This What's Gonna Happen, When Is It Gonna Happen? What might I know? What must I do? What might I hope for?

The rebellious Labancz, he's the key? Let's face it? Because he's gotta have his victory so that later, by keeping strictly within official channels, of course, he may report it to his imperial highness? It makes me puke? It's one of those infantile, mid-life excesses? Order and discipline at all cost?

I want more of the same?

It's dark inside my mouth, I'm scared?

I can't go on like this, for chrissakes, can't you get it through my thick skull?

The subjugating Labancz has a face that is *crooked*? Depends on how you look at it? There's the Labancz that's a *slow draw* and the Labancz that's a *fast draw*? – Should our Good Lord so ordain that we in a castle find ourselves incarcerated where every son o'god is busied with finding ways of plundering in our innards, craving the little we possess while we *openly* and *publicly* declare ourselves to be a freedom-loving Kurucz as we stand in the spacious castle yard in our torn and bloodied linen shirt, but without calling undue attention to ourselves, one this way, another that, there's enough and some to go around, up above on the circular open galleries and Italian-style porticoes men keep a lethargic watch, the hands still fumbling with the saddles, nailing boards, wielding axes, flaying, sewing, keeping generally busy, the women are more high-strung and amuse themselves with bloodthirsty cries, *string him up by his third leg!* and when they whoop and bawl and the men smack their bottoms they take no offence; conversely, bending forward and pressing their ample groins against the balustrade, which is exactly the right height, and working in minuscule circles invisible to the naked eye they wriggle, writhe, twist, thrust and hump rhythmically? Or was it more like a light touch?

If the fickle finger of fate brings a subjugating Labancz your way that's *quick on the draw*, there's no time for shilly-shallying, the puny fellow's a greenhorn, he don't mess around, ignorant of time and effervescence, bang, bang, you're dead, and before you can say jack be nimble, they cover your emaciated shoulders with the threadbare loden coat of martyrdom while he, turning on his side, is already snoring, dreaming the dream of the just?

The Labancz that's *slow on the draw* will not tolerate such frivolous and cocky little shrieks, and through the prohibition of the grabbing of the ample buttocks, he imparts a certain solemnity to the proceedings, helpless as he may be in face of the minuscule circles invisible to the naked eye, the result being a touch of cynicism? Our Labancz's arms are crossed in front of his chest, he is standing with legs apart, knowing his own mind yet timid, too, his speech *simpatico*, polished, *words are spoken*, slowly, wisely, without haste, yet *leading somewhere*? In the lean-to the soldiers are playing cards, they are ill at ease, their cocked guns, faithful *puli* dogs, resting at their feet, clubs are trumps? By the balustrades the coquettish ladies are quieting down now, panting slowly, sweetly, their rosy cheeks, glistening with saliva, part, *like orphans, we are standing in the belly of the region*, for an instant this just about moves us to tears, but only for an instant, oh how we love everything, ourselves especially, our subjugating Labancz is dependable and unruffled, he's not taken in by our amateurish pranks, he goes about his business unperturbed, his intonation professionally importunate, and this resourceful crumbling-spiralling, give-a-little take-a-little handling of time quickly leads to that blessed flash in the pan? In the end, though, it grows chilly, the bright stars appear in the dark firmament, the guard is changed, like phantoms, strolling soft and tardy, the women are *off*, and we are free to sit, sticking to the matted straw?

On this day the weather is mild?

The *squeamish* type, he carries his nose in the air, wiping his hands repeatedly, why're our swords rusty, why're our chains rusty, our blood, phew!, in short, he thinks he's of better mettle?

The *adventurous* type, if he so much as stoops to speak, well, my heart skips a beat, what has the old war-horse got up his sleeve this time?

And the *domestic* type, sitting on his oafish mare, he brandishes his sword, reaping what he can, as if he were on a pre-season package tour here? Per cent?

But you gotta go easy? The Kurucz mustn't forget his manners?
I'm no fool to go tell this brand-new rascal, my honoured imperial adversary, this beribboned, purulent asshole whom I greet with my meek demeanour, tripping tongue, shallow intellect, pure heart and true brotherly love, may God save him – as long as he sees fit; in short to tell him what's what (what's-what and what's-not-what!), because in his zeal he might not be loath to organise a sort of mini-competition, chalking it all up, just so he can prove he's the only one by whose side it's going to hit me? While I'm blinded by fury?

Or if I'm not blinded, and I see my fearless opponent's rather anxious but well-meaning exertion, i.e., the fact that he does not spare himself (by not sparing us), his hand slippery with blood, his face playfully streaked with soot – in short, I cannot get myself to carp about how democracy this and democracy that, why wound his pride so openly? Time is a great good friend? You get to know the other better?

All of which can take a discreet shape as well as a brutally open one?
Types of fear: from a subtle quaking in your boots to a cautious ranting and raving? Exhibiting all the symptoms in accordance with the latest scientific findings? The subjugating Labancz beats his tail in delight at the sight of social discipline thus shrunk down to size, which, with a little practice, can be conjured up at the snap of a finger?

Let the son of a bitch think he's the great *Zampano*?
That's one? And then, our countenance light blue, we tug nervously at our trousers and bend, puking, over the cool and
likewise light-blue concavity of the tiles? Not a chance? A Magyar's a Magyar's a Magyar's a Magyar? Beaten but not bowed?
Summer hath flown the coop and now you discard me like a box
of used matches? Forehead slashed, hair bloodsoaked, eyes to the
ground rooted? The autumn leaves they are a-falling, crabbed
age doth with solemnity ask what the future's got in store for the
young?

**Some take to weeping afterwards? The magpie, said the larkspur, is
no friend of the larkspur?**
The hawk-nosed German S.O.B. thinks, from the point of view
of it *hitting* you, there's nothing like *doing you in* and if it should
work, if they do us in and it hits us, then everything is *hunky-
dory*?

While our bosom pals don't realise how in this way they are
themselves erecting walls *for themselves* at the base of which they
can go and fight like heroes till their arms go numb and their
spirits are depleted? At all events, the choice should be based on
the conviction that what we have is what we want, and on the
freedom that that's how things stand? A cold wind is a-blowing?

Again: regardless? Regardless, the Labancz inside us rages with
superior ease, pushing and pulling, grabbing, twisting, advancing,
circling, his pungent perfumes, like the smell of horseradish,
tickle the nose, and his ill-shaven face cuts deep wounds into us?

And then, *en garde*? Time for a tad o' swashbucklin'? Mortally wounded, our horses collapse beneath us, paying next to no heed to the IPB (Irrational Pull of the Bridle), the good comrade obligingly sinks his imperial claws into our pimple-infested necks, we are as downy and fragile as a doe in the reeds, I like to know we are in such close proximity, to hear his terrified wheezing, his panting, his groaning, the claw-like curvature of his fingers, to feel that Labancz-like throbbing in which it is not difficult to discern the depth and breadth of a bold universal plan, a blueprint, a scheme, as if the very stars were pulsating in the blood which I am shedding?

To be in close proximity? Our cheeks touch and we grab each other by the scruff of the neck, this is the Free-for-All phase which follows hard upon the Give-a-Little, Take-a-Little, Push-and-Pull phase, he bites me, I lick my salty blood, feeling the traces of his pearly whites with the tip of my tongue, with a firm grip on each other's flesh we do a flip over tranquil streams, mounds, meadows, the cement powder evenly settled on the blades of grass, over mud piles, concrete playgrounds, pedestrian crossings, legally binding one-way streets, past boarded-up fountains and splash pools, flattening out pearly mole-hill mounds, exhausted, each listens to the other's heart beating, breathing each other's air, with muscles tense and flexed, so we can drop off and slumber in each other's arms, lullaby-baby, an idle ant crawling over our cheek? The world's one universal embrace, we can lie to our heart's content as long as there's breath left in us?

I lie as low as cow dung in the grass?
We are alone, desperately alone? This is what I will mean by saying that the Kurucz is condemned to freedom? You, sir, are lying sprawled on your bed, whispering to no one in particular:

verminiferous, flea-ridden, grubby, foul, abominable, heathen, slave, Magyar, fascist, *insipid*, wretched, infamous, bestial, loathsome, vile, abject, base, putrid, filth, pus, muck, whore, poxy, filthy, heinous, rank, sordid, contemptible, harlot, trollop, whore, strumpet? – *Puppentheater*, as the more astute of the Labancz would say? And if it should hit the Labancz before it hits you, madame, will you, madame, be piqued? Your stomach in knots, the first thing that pops into your head: so what, no big deal, it was *neat* while it lasted; *but then you dig in your heels and refuse to see why you should be taking it so calmly?*

When the bastard should lick every one of his ten gnarled, fluxuous fingers for having gotten someone like you?

Life is delightful? Our sense of justice is lively, frolicsome as a filly, while we ourselves are radiant, our five senses in a whirl, the short vests of the young misses and maidens stretched tight across their bosoms, the prim pearl buttons can hardly bear their flattering burden, in the whirlwind the skirts rise, the forbidden, dangerous and sweet terrain of round kneecaps and rosy thighs revealed to our wicked eyes, the floor virtually steaming with the dust, the boots and silk slippers pound on the floor, the profuse sweat breaking through the shield of the beauty products, the noses tremble squeamishly, out on the clearing they are jumping over gentle fires, the white folk, tender and mature alike, their legs flung wide apart so they can warm themselves in the meantime, the moon like some thorn beckoning, rearing its hind legs in the sky, arm in arm we surge forward over the rifts we have cut into the body of our beloved city, flooding the boulevards, the avenues, the prospekts and one-way side-roads, and weeping, we sing the national anthem, while out on the open terraces the guests, tied to their creaky, sparkling-white wicker chairs, jump to their feet and join us with their chairs stuck to them? Our national anthem is the most beautiful and saddest anthem in the world, all eyes are filled with tears, and strangers kiss each other on the cheek?

Variations? Flat on our back, so we don't even know who stirs on top of us, or wandering about on all fours, closely watched by our ferocious and determined enemies, our knees badly scraped by the horse-hair stuffing, terrified, we repeatedly tense our buttock muscles and though we know the good fortune that awaits us, still, the simple fact of it happening surprises us anew – 'what's this?' 'oh?' 'could it really *be*?' as we stare, naïve and innocent, into the huge oval tray of silver that serves us as a mirror?

The asymmetry of our eyes imparts a look of mild untrustworthiness, a sort of sly-fox look, a firm want of responsibility, even our most ruthless adversary gone, yes, indeed, who with his ripped-open chest, his still warm insides obligingly tumbling from him, his maimed limbs, jerking, severed arms and legs, could have offered a solution to our psychological problems; we sit at the foot of a plum tree, the somniferous fruit disappearing from under our hand, we sink into ourselves, the viper's bugloss creaking in the bad wind, the same old story, the same old story, hurrahs like sighs coming from the distance, a plum falls, suck me dry, someone whispers coolly from a nearby bush, light a cigarette, turn your back, sleep, old boy, tomorrow is another day?

They have raped my face?
They have raped my neither too tall nor too slight frame, they have raped my long, brawny features, they have raped my black

and twinkling eyes, largish, hooked nose, largish ears and long arms, they have raped the toes on my foot, the nails ugly, unsightly coils, possibly because of the narrow boots, they have raped my thin, waspish waist, my lovely, fleshy, rounded cheeks, my neck, my throat, my thighs, my buttocks, they have raped it?

So why bang our head against the wall, for godssake? *Forget the past, start life anew, sweet memories goodbye, adieu?* The sky is blue again above, for I am serene as a dove? Self-realisation's here, tra-la? TIME HAS STOPPED, *tra-la la-la?* The mute stars, how they do twinkle in the sky, *tra-la la-la la-kla-la?* You keep mum and I keep mum?

'Go wash up.' 'I want you.'?
O ye abjects fools racked by inner torments of the heart, o ye pitiful half-wits, sobbing and distressed? It gives you something to think about? *Du musst dein Leben ändern* – you must change your life: who the devil except for the honourable group-captain can say this?

Let us talk of oppression and revolution? *Ad notam*: let us talk about whores: your mother, how is she? We swear by the *?????* of the Magyars (fabricating untranslatable puns about their god?).

Revolution? What revolution? A newspaperman's gimmick, a journalist's trick? Most Labancz are under-informed, they stand grinning by their multitude of horses, shouting who goes there? It's the same old story: the subjugating Labancz wants to *give it* to you, the poor freedom-loving Kurucz wants it to *hit* him, but so what? What's *new* in this? The grass crushed underfoot, the sheet drenched and crumpled, but where's the revolution? It's

just another PR stunt, accomplishment fixation, just another
market opened up? Some sort of coloured something around the
neck, a kerchief, perhaps, or shiny medals on the chest, but that's
not *that*, not the well-wrought new man with his beauty and
freedom, just some fashionable fad at best?

The New Passion just a bag of tricks, out of the frying pan into
the fire, cropped Magyar *mente* coats, hair shaved up to there,
pretty blue eyes: that's all it takes, that's all it means? Discos? *On
my face a smile that never varies 'cause life ain't nothin' but a bowl
'a cherries?* If in order to flaunt himself the Kurucz parades his
horse along the embankment on a fine summer's day and his horse
neighs, may I remind you: a horse laugh is still a laugh, don't
forget; he storms through the green, tranquil afternoon, while
the Labancz wriggles himself out of his filthy hovel, bleary-eyed,
he rearranges the lines of his wrinkled face overgrown with a
thick stubble, and they come to grips – well, what of it? *You are
free*, the indolent beribboned German whispers leaning against
his big, scrawny mare – but that's just the shit of it, dontcha see?
Because around these parts if the Kurucz follows events with a
sober mind, and having adopted the well-oiled model of passion
and manly verve from the Labancz, it's not freedom he'll be
wanting, but to find his own way, overgrown with weed and
oakum as it may be?

Who're you kidding? Let's not lose our head? Up our own
mother, the Labancz can go do us a favour that'll make our head
spin down the rivers Drava and up the Vág now in Yugoslavia,
but then in southern Hungary? It wouldn't even surprise us if
he were to end up scoring against his own team? We're not
new-born calves? Just born yesterday? Young 'uns, says the old
tobacconist who is missing both legs from the trunk down, look,

you gotta pay for it every time, see? A pack a' gum and sunshades? We're no better than we should be? The Kurucz might be more prepossessing than the Labancz, but so what, they share a common culture, language and past (*e.g.*, the breadbasket of Europe), but some are just filthy pigs, and that's that? Takes a whore to know a whore?

You, sir, are in the habit of making courageous pronouncements, passionate, gutsy, no-nonsense statements that freeze the very air in the bosoms of the crowds streaming out of the dark metro, the dark tunnel, and they exchange a look (as they *advance*) as if to say, can one *really*? could this too be all right now?, while sensing their mute question, your features ironed out, you cast your eyes up up and away as if you were the main character in a promotional reaping poster of the not too distant past, yes, friends, this too is just fine now? The atmosphere sizzles, and if you also had to pay *on your way out*, if those were the rules, the proper procedure, the price of not using the metro, well, then, this time no one would pay, while the men at the turnstiles would *wink* at this libertarianism either because they would prove broad-minded or because they would know they are helpless in the face of the ecstatic, *surging crowds*, and so they would not grab you by the ear, they would not give you a dressing-down, they would not haul you over the coals or drag you through the mire, they would not cook your goose, chastise you in public, or read you the Riot Act?

No, sirree? We are not slapped around any more, we are exempted from having our ears boxed, from being spanked, grabbed by the scruff of our neck and rapped over the knuckles, it's *passé*, we have stopped begging, trembling, for our lives, we are not wrapped in rugs or in still wet, though drying sheets, we do not get our

clenched teeth forced apart with a jack-knife so they can stuff
our mouth full of salt, the soles of our feet are not swollen and
bloody, nor are they black-and-blue, water is not made to trickle
drop by drop on our shaven head, no abscesses throb under our
armpit, they do not dig their heels into our stomach and our nails
too have gone relatively unharmed, and if they are not, we have
only ourselves to blame, they do not break our balls any more,
thank God, our testicles are healthy and regular and are up to
par, brimming with health, our insides are not being ripped out
either, is that a fact or is that a fact?

You can have too much of a bad thing —

Let us wake to it being fondled? To the realisation that there is
no accursed silence that'd make it worth our while to button
up, nor the hue and cry that'd filthy us without accomplishing
something; let us wake to a gentle stirring, to the warm melody
of our outstretched limbs, let our yellow butterfly blanket ripple
softly, playfully, like a small pond?[26] Let us long for the open sea,
let us long to be in the windswept puddles after an ebb-tide,
we'd gladly tumble around in them and feel a sensuous lack of
fulfilment? Let us hide under the blanket and meditate on the
nature of the dark, let us breathe deeply, relishing the pungent,
stale air, and in the distance let us lift the blanket with our toe
and let there be a *spot* of light there?

---

[26] The picture: a soft, light, yellow, warm, fluffy butterfly blanket on a wide bed.
Lying under it is a young brunette. Drahosch? The man gives her a look of disgust
(?), pulls the butterfly blanket off her, like a dishrag. The woman is missing both legs
from the trunk down. MOTTO: HELL'S BELLS.

Why shouldn't we consider ourselves for a change? Why shouldn't we locate adjectives? *Horribile dictu*: predicates? What reason could there be for burying the initiatives that'd make us latch on to exciting, as yet unknown directions?

But as long as the present schizoid dichotomy exists between official and non-official, public and private, authentic reality and inauthentic reality, our moral imperative of playing the role of dam or source or tampon in the flow of the world's affairs falls to the wayside and crestfallen, we harp instead on the ethos of the non-presence of power while life becomes commercialised to the extreme, more and more substantial portions of our private lives being invaded, while we gradually lose the capacity to recognise the profound and painful significance of it all?

Is this what I am? Is this my conscience, my bad conscience, are these my national feelings, my sense of justice? See the bond of social responsibility and my voluptuous plump buttocks, all my very own *territorial waters*, and if anybody, a villain with and without a country, a good for nothing, distinguished, conceited weathercock should attempt to sail on said waters against my will, well, then, baby, don't spare the rod?

Why shouldn't I ask questions? Purposefully unwhittled questions, to make my triumph seem all the greater when the time comes? Or would you prefer questions *whittled into shape*? Come to think of it, are you, personally, of the right *whittle*? Would you like to be? Do you know the expression: where-whittle? Well? A kind of wine? A musical instrument, possibly some sort of pipe? Cowardly submission? None of the above?

Miska Halassi is dead, his throat slashed, his face cleft in twain by a sabre, the bluish blood adhering to his beard like a piece of lead?

Besides, the way of the future is the way of quality, from the humble hip-hip-hurrah to the greater, more complex manly verve, and I am not referring to any technological hanky-panky either, playing the bass tuba, the funnel pen, petting, attack from the flanks, newspapers? Not that these things are devoid of interest? I am thinking, rather, of the difference between a sapling and an old, portly tree with spreading branches, thinking, in the case of the latter, of the form and structure, which is always unique, one of a kind?

Are you one of a kind? A sapling? Or portly, with spreading branches? But you learned early on, too early, alas, what's what? Came on four wheels but left on foot? Ashes to ashes, dust to dust more times than you would care to count? Being a wolf in sheep's clothing, you strut around with your balls pulling in two directions, just to make doubly sure? *Life here is but a masquerade, why don't you come join in the parade? There is no yesterday, tomorrow is another day? Well fella, am I your fella?* Oh? Is that so? A weary habitué of music halls? How're the ladies fair? Who will guarantee their safety? You?

Who're you trying to kid? Not even that one single *lady* you were with on the local train? The cause: a certain shitting in the pants? Or the ancient character of our people, which people is prey to doubt, though its scepticism is not cynical but sober, not a cynical bitterness but a shrug of the shoulder, a melancholy capitulation at best, mitigated by a well-intentioned, hoity-toity humour? It all depends whether you look at it *with love and from within*, or from without? As a rule, the faults and virtues are identical, only the point of view differs?

Our homeland? By definition: a unique formation on a circumscribed terrain; today: good times in a garlanded landscape? In which case, what are we to do? First and foremost, take account of what László Németh[27] formulated thus: 'To belittle something may be all right as a *judgement*, but it will not do as an *attitude*. Our country may be backward as a *place*, an object of pity, but as the chosen spot for our actions it is the most important place on earth. The place to which we are born must guide our actions as surely as the nature which we have created.'

And what next?

Take off your glasses? My friend? We do trust you so? You might as well come clean? We know everything anyhow? Come, come? Why this show of obstinacy, without a shadow of a doubt did you run *fit to burst* after the last local? Because the Municipal Transport Authority is as reliable as death and taxes?

You are up on the open platform, panting and wheezing, you couldn't hold it back if you tried, the local is the same old construction, only the green different, the ugly lady is standing in a corner, leaning against that *mysterious wheel* which had always intrigued you so, not knowing its purpose, what it was for, and this lack of purpose – like those threatening letters in which you can't discover the threat, the letters are so much lacking in direction they are almost *pleasingly* whimsical, until they frighten

---

[27] Németh (1901–1975): the same as Gyula Illyés, but different. Like Illyés, the scion of peasants who engaged in the traditional forms of the novel of realism. But unlike Illyés, he was immersed in the socialist view of the world *up to here.*

you half to death – increased the value of the wheel? (You thought of it as a wheel, it was the obvious thing to do, but reality intervened to shatter your dream in the shape of the rails?)

Timid that you are, you'd rather gaze at the mirror-image of the girl, this more remote, obscure and improbable countenance; the *mediated* proximity calms your nerves, you do not feel the weight of the responsibility which your solitude imposes upon you, a weight tailored to you, while you adjust your long, yellow knitted scarf confusedly bunched up from the running; even the knot is not properly attended to, you can neither tie or knot it nor fling it over your shoulder with verve? You hated the girl and pleaded with her for her favours *inside?*

The winters of our unfounded discontents are multiplying like rats?
Lying at a right angle to the wheel, the short but massive stick-like crank of the wheel sinks into the girl's thigh, your association of ideas is lewd and vulgar, a gully appears on her coat like a rubber ball that's been pushed in but on which it is plain to see that before long it will win back its primary and very real shape, and all this *sneaks* not a little *tension* into the material? (You had similar thoughts once when a woman said to you: *my clitoris is about to explode?* A serious misapprehension? You shot wide of the mark? Or conversely?)

But all your little tricks are for naught, your hopes dashed, seeing that you are yellow through and through and there's nothing you want as much as to run for your chicken-shit life? It stands to reason? Behind a woman's skirt, that's where you belong? Or conversely, it's what you're trying to cut and run from? There? Under the bell? The multifarious, base, shirking movement is already stirring inside you, your foot stirring on the grubby floor, a willow-sword inside a gilt sheath? Not to worry, though: swords of all kinds are at a far remove from sheaths of all kinds, far as you're concerned?

Your pants, is that where you wear your heart? Absolutely? Pit-a-pat? Oh, young sir, so *refined*, just listen to your little heart pound and pound? Your hand resting in your pocket, or on the delicate curve of your scarf, your head or just your lashes stirring in resignation, yes, you are about to move inside the car when with a clumsy, ungainly gesture the girl leaves her corner and without further ado sinks her watery gaze into you? You want to flee to the gully of the thighs to see what next, the firm grasp of the crank weakening, you search for the brashness in the girl's eyes but can find no trace of it? Because of the light? Let's not go into it? You're no sugar and cream yourself? Just sugar?

The lady is not only unsightly but repulsive? A harridan, a toad, a Caliban? Plain Jane? With some cheap talk, milk from the cow with the iron tail, you approach, her response one of overwhelming joy? Now it is your turn to lean against the handle, but seeing the obligatory gully on your *own* thigh you are terrified, you feel queasy, even slightly nauseous, your grip on reality weakened about who is who, the distasteful St Vitus's dance of the interchange of identities is about to commence, you being the lady and so on and so forth, but being the more sensible of the two, the girl leaves you no time for such self-indulgence, *bagatelle*, she talks instead about her work, the peculiarities of the wages paid to weaving women, the many absurdities; the irony and self-irony behind her loose phraseology and sloppy handling of words which must have been part of her nature all along take you by surprise, you did not think her capable? Her face is a profusion of repulsive blackheads and not only in the excusable spots either, at the base of the nose, for instance, but also on the open terrain of her face and concealed among the thin hairs of her brows and on her forehead, with big black points in the centre? She is dirty, that's your impression, *rent material*, which doesn't worry you in the least?

Events are coming to a head? In one of the easy, deserted turns in the road your knee touches hers – are you cartilage-*liable*? – desperate, you hope that this effrontery, which had its roots in a chance occurrence, will be met by a justified and firm rebuff; but the girl's description of the treacherous male mentality of the foremen grows more heated, at the bottom of which, obviously, lies, so says the girl, *impotento grosso*, and she laughs and presses your knee between her own? Which is so absurd, you take your hand from yourself right away?

You put your arm around the girl, resting your head on her shoulder because you want to avoid kissing her no matter what, having to cop a kiss, a superfluous, personal detour, not that it gets you much, the girl's hair being sour and foul-smelling, a sticky, stiff ringlet flaps against your cheek, it is like an armour, it does not cascade, it is beating, flailing and slamming against you, bang-bang (an apolitical iron curtain), cutting the sight of her nape, with which you were hoping to amuse yourself in relative safety, off from view?

The girl chatters non-stop, you later admire this clever, *benign* psychologising, so then, the unrelenting locks of hair are in your face like so many sharp shards when what do you feel all of a sudden? You feel that this person of dubious morals, this dear, dear soul, has reached under your raglan overcoat, manoeuvring dextrously right under your pullover and, to cut a long story short, her hand is resting on your belly? In summary: *hot feminine hands are fondling your belly on the deserted local train?* Holding your breath, you keep your limp hand on the girl's waist, then, to reciprocate, you would like to slip your hand through the mysterious slit in the girl's coat, but your noble intentions are thwarted by the cause of your noble intentions as you bump into the girl's hand and so, in your frustration, you *lurk towards* the girl's buttocks, her intimate derrière, crude ass, refined rear parts, charming posterior, funny bunnies, uncouth hunkers, beauteous bum, precious fundament, seatie, sternie, childish patootie, oh, how you'd like to play tootsie-footsie with the little floosie? Through the coat, with a goodly number of detours?

Just the same, the moment is significant (orbital?), for it happens to be the first time they (strangers) have actually touched your virile member *officially*; after all, we cannot regard as such the former simply *playful* diddles, whether through the agency of your siblings or your mother, or even your just mutating school chums? It hit you? Like the world about to explode? Like the world converging on one gleaming, brilliant spot of light, then exploding in earnest? A groin-explosion? Anarchists? Resignation and abject fear? Red Brigades between your legs? You bite down on your lip, drawing blood to stop you from screaming, while the girl grins discreetly and points to your handkerchief?

Time, which deserves to be taken more seriously, is running out on the two of you, but you don't give a damn? Then the ending, like some insipid horror story, because when the local comes to a screeching halt at the St Stephen Colony the lady looks out and shouting *jesus*!!! tosses you from her? A couple of suspicious-looking guys from the outskirts, with long side-locks? All of a sudden she turns vindictively cold? Don't get off, just don't get off, she pleads, on the defensive, the tone of her voice tainted by her (why beat about the bush) betrayal, because she is about to sacrifice you *without a second thought* to save herself, throwing you to the dogs, or whatever?

Don't you dare get off *now*, mister, or I frig your member so you won't feel like going to school no more?

Upon reflection, you thought of this eventuality as a major catastrophe? That they might rob you of your fair share of knowledge? Or was it the cold again? Notwithstanding, the girl, as she nervously and cowardly tugs at her coat and cursing under her breath scampers off, looks back, her fleeting smile a crix-crux of meanings, though all she says is, well, mister?

We're as silent as a frog lurking in a cesspool? On the City Park lake the girls broke into clumsy titters of laughter, but when a boat appeared from under the bridge with a gang of curly-haired boys, it hit you how even these second-rate smiles were not meant for you? Fate, you were convinced at the time, had given you a bum steer? You wandered around the shore, with plenty of frogs, alive each and every one? Life is short, but misery makes it seem a whole lot longer?

You clutched your treasure, the toad lying low in the family matchbox, passionately closer? A fairy-tale twist starring a beautiful princess would have come in handy just then? Which the beast must have felt, because it began to stir?

Throbbing, the toad is throbbing?

But then, like a wicked anti-hero did you fling the disguised, reactionary lady into the red enamelled pot, slapped on the lid and lit the fire without further ado? The loathsome colourless mass, the toad, the lady, gave in without a fight as far as the removal of the soft parts was concerned, then you put the clammy, loathsome bones out on the windowsill to dry in the sun? But as luck would have it (and like the poet says) it was soon gone with the wind?

The series of daring sacrifices, the mighty efforts and moral deep ends, all in vain? You made your way to school beaten and melancholy? Watchword: spleen? Abandoning yourself to grief? Or grace?

When you and your classmates entered the classroom, you were in the habit of throwing your caps on the floor, thus freeing your hands; it had to be slapped under the bench from the threshold so it would bounce against the wall and whip up as much dust as it possibly could; this was the latest *rage* among you? The adventurous story of the catching of the toad was met with horrendous interest followed by laughter, the biology teacher stroked your noddle, but you would not compromise? You are a defiant dog?

Were other modifications made in the narrative? Not in the least.
With a bad case of cold feet but proud, you continue your journey till you reach the last stop on the local? Meanwhile you use your ingenuity to rehearse a number of ways they might dip this or that into you up to the hilt? You wait for the first early-morning train back? Your heart aches for someone? Growing more and

more insensate, you sit on a cheerless bench, your groins made of stone?

Empty? Are you empty? Numbness and lethargy as far as the eye can see? But is this any way of defining anything? Or are you not that noble-minded? Yes, you are that noble-minded, certainly?

You strike up a conversation and soon find yourself discussing the future with some young army recruits? Talking non-stop, *bitching*, coming to unlikely conclusions? About what the Kurucz wants? We want the load of our lives to be lighter, we want our roads to be cleaner, and the boulevards, the motorways, the side-streets, the lanes, the serendipitous squares born of the meeting-place of neutral streets, and Heroes Square, too, and the alleys, the avenues, the galleries running around the inner courtyards of old apartment houses, the bases of the balustrades, the public stairwells, the bus stops, the toilet seats, our necks, our backs, our groins, the area around our Achilles' heels, we want our imagination to grow in scope, to be strangers no more to courage and daring, like Hašek's Good Soldier Švejk, desperate, daring and attractive, we want to walk around barefoot in the larger than large rooms of old stately mansions, we want to be together, and we want to trust each other, and we want to be alone, and may the devil take our never-ending string of courtesies, our reserved good breeding and intractable self-discipline, we want to cast off our masks of sanctity, we want more truth and passion, we want the mother-fucking Labancz to be more than a colossal pie in the sky ideology that strives to play at democracy, we want a hardy welcome to find a hardy welcome, may God bless you and keep you, my sweet, sweet friend?

Don't work yourself into a frenzy, old boy?

To live is to . . .?

To live is to waver between certain possibilities, to live is to think ourselves *fatefully* strong in the practice of democracy, to live is to choose our own destiny in the world, nor is there a single moment when this vigilance of ours can relax; even if we are discouraged, allowing things to take their own course, we are making a choice, that of not choosing; but possibly this is the starting point of life, because to be alive is to feel lost, and since this is the honest truth, to know that to be alive is to feel lost, he who accepts this is already on his way to finding himself, he has already begun to discover the true reality of his being, is already standing on firm ground; instinctively, like a shipwrecked man will he go in search of something to get hold of, and this tragic, determined and absolutely authentic glance with which he searches for his liberation will guide him through the labyrinth of life; only these are the authentic thoughts: the thoughts of a shipwrecked man, the rest is rhetoric, posturing, self-delusion; he who does not feel himself truly lost will be lost without reprieve, he will never find himself, will never discover his own reality?

So then, bitching, talking non-stop, the young recruits wave, *adieu mon petit* lieutenant of the guard, the crowded car is heavy with cigarette smoke, you sneak a look at the cards of the card players, some have decidedly rotten luck, a whippersnapper with a weary face requests, would you kindly get the fuck out of his way, don't you know you are bad luck?

Having disembarked, we stand around for a long time, righting our limp scarf with an involuntary gesture; and we stand in the neon-lit dawn like an old man? In a sky chiselled smooth by the wind, like a pane of Formica, the stars show like silver flakes, tarnished now and again by the yellow gleam of a revolving light? Perfumes of spice and warm stone are wafted on the breeze? A couple of streets down a car must have skidded on the wet pavement, then silently drives away, and in its wake distant, confused cries rend the air? Then, like a dense veil slowly falling from the starry sky, silence returns?

The poplars reaching for the sky are our fellow passengers, at the foot of the tall, luxuriant pines the bit of quivering snow appears ludicrous, the faded forest litter jutting through, while on the branches of the scant thicket the flakes of snow tremble like a fancy net that's seen better days? The tenacious bindweed creeps up the trunks of the nearby birches, the trees, the grasses, the weeds do not waste away, the mosses, the green veins of the wet soil do not waste away? A velvety sound hovers in the air?

In the privacy of our homes tears come to our eyes, and we are shaken by mute sobs? This weeping ascends from the heart of the sleeping house like a flower sprouting from the heart of silence?

The morning comes to us drop by drop, like chloroform on the operating table, the snow is crisp, our clothes are fluttering on the big, portly trees, the robes, the short *mente* coats, the kerchiefs, the dolmans; it is dawning, and we question and we doubt, in the distance men on horseback are galloping with majestic and provocative *sang froid*, Hungary is not of the past but of the future?

It must to be —

IV
(the engineer of the soul)[28]

> *I have nothing to say and I am*
> *saying it . . .*
> *and that is poetry.*
> *(John Cage)*

> *The handing over of the travel*
> *documents carried with it the same*
> *kind of threat. Ex.: 'Here you are,*
> *sir.'*

> *As he watched the tiny warships*
> *through the square lens, for some*
> *reason he thought of celery —*
> *pleasantly fragrant celery on top of*
> *a portion of beefsteak cooked over hot*
> *charcoal.*
> *(Akutagawa Ryunosuke)*

The stuffed swan
When I am working, (. . . .) thought, my heart overflows with the

---

[28] Stalin's famous designation of the writer.

milk of human kindness. And for a light-headed, rash and fleeting moment he really did feel he was the engineer of the soul. He stood waving at the retreating cab as it disappeared with deep, melancholy lyricism through the descending fog, mysteriously as those gigantic ocean liners from whose belly the sound of a never-ending fox-trot used to issue, then with the toe of his boot he kicked the hardened clumps of snow and started for home when, not even halfway there, he burst into tears, a surprise. The tears flowed calm and even,[29] a regular trickle, but though he thought of the ebb-tide of his tears as a sign that he was gaining gradual relief, the uneasy congestion he felt inside would not let up. On the contrary. This was him, the stuffed swan.

The shop-window dummy

He[30] wanted to live so thoroughly unbridled that if he should die, there'd be no regrets. And yet he continued to live modestly with his foster parents and aunt. His life had two sides – a light side and a dark side. Once he saw a dummy in the shop for European clothing, and he was struck by the thought that he was really very much like that shop-window dummy. But his subconscious, his other ego, had already described this mood some time ago in one of his earlier short stories.

[29] 'We are living in a new non-literary culture.' (Susan Sonntag)
[30] 'I write in the third person singular. It makes me feel safe. I hope I won't die quite so soon.' P. Esterházy.

What is today's prose writer like?

Today's prose writer is a dour, endearing figure of a man. He rarely lifts his gaze off the ground, bizarre, neurotic, nightmarish, in search of his breakfast; when earnest college girls call him up he blushes and accepts their pleasurable invitations with a bad conscience; he loiters about, studying the artful dust-balls tumbling around the sidewalk, the pedestrian crossing and the traffic light above: if his spirits are low that is why his spirits are low, if he spirits are high, then that's why; then, when the dusk, always mysterious, falls, he pussyfoots his way to a certain house known to one and sundry, though they pretend they've never heard of it, *he sneaks a look*, and while he watches the red-haired monkey taking possession of the frightfully beautiful princess who puts up almost no resistance at all he grabs his own member; then he goes home, pours himself a glass of red wine and proceeds to note down everything he's seen. He tries to find himself a woman for the night, but he hasn't got much time because like a swift flood does the moment of breakfast approach.

What is today's prose writer like?

Today's prose writer is a lonely figure of a man. Day after day does he observe with a sense of wonder and elation the people around him, his wife, his sons and daughters, plus his various friends of both sexes. Sometimes they go to the outskirts of town, sit on chequered blankets and cook wild meats. Sometimes it even happens that the entire company ups and goes to filch cherries. These are the simple pleasures of summertime. In the spring, the sun shines in through the window. In the fall, he watches the high school girls from a distance – plus the fluttering golden leaves. The winters are pristine. In this way each season holds something in store for him.

What is today's prose writer like?

Today's prose writer is a quiet figure of a man. On the other hand he is highly sensitive and cannot stand to 'hear to the end' the buzz and burr of the hair dryer, even if it is a question of his own hair, as a consequence of which he is constantly suffering from a head cold and sniffles through the nose; in short, he is sensitive, but at least he is not the shouting type. He does a lot of thinking, though. He thinks about God, the nation, and other things besides. As he comes and goes, he can't get over the absurdity of the world he sees. 'I can't believe it,' he says with a shake of the head. But when he thinks of all the things that are yet going to happen to him, his heart rejoices.

But that's not what I mean to say. But that he is quiet, lies low, at best sits and dawdles, satisfied if he is able to fill the sheet of paper lying in front of him. His main characteristics: a disdain of defeatism, self-adulation, solipsism, cruelty, puns, faint-heartedness, a loathing of self-loathing, *ergo* of himself; feeling sorry for those that feel sorry for themselves, thereby saving himself from its sweet excesses. Or whatever. To a man like him life's no joke by halves. But from time to time he breaks out anyhow, shouting. 'I have no love for this intoxicating, loathsome and maddening world and I am bent on changing it.'

What is today's prose writer like?

Today's prose writer is the kind of man whose life is the kind of life that doesn't progress from one place to the next. Consequently, the novel does not progress from here to there either. Which means that the action is more like an arch . . . Which means that he, too, thumbs through 19th-century novels, taking account with irresponsible, loving care of the successful efforts to enhance the illusion of truth. In which case, what is his own novel like? It is like him, of course, it is like his life and ours, that certain something around which we stand loitering, watching it with an apprehensive grimace, yet it is as if it weren't ours at all. Yes, it runs around in circles, like a chicken without its head, and I am appalled to see how at times it weeps, at others it cries.

Conservative values
'The world is fragmented.' 'Indeed it is.' Then: 'But I don't think man is any further removed from God than at any other time.' Leaving the municipal public library built in the exaggerated style of the Schinkel school, but already finding himself in the park, he gave the woman in a hat who was walking her poodle a cocky sort of look. She was rich, *loaded*, and clearly unaccustomed to such insolence, or if she was, it was not her custom to *let it lie*. They stopped, whereupon he noticed how the woman had inadvertantly spread her legs so her thighs would not rub together in the sweltering heat.

Sunrise
He got up early. His trouser legs were wet from the dew. In this he could even detect a personal triumph of sorts, a state of mind in which he might have even accepted without squeamishness the praises of his dubious schoolmasters.

(. . . .) was picking at the ground in front of the house because the day before an old gentleman wearing an armband had rung the doorbell and with penitent resolve reminded him of the approaching holiday. Surely it was *no secret*, even to him, and would he *kindly* sweep the sidewalk so that, as they say, the old

man said, (. . . .)'s house should not be the object of talk, *literally
speaking*. This reference to literature alone would have sufficed,
but the People's Coalition, too, might drop by to do a little spot-
checking, the man added. He nodded eagerly. He felt he should
be nodding eagerly. The old man took off on his heavy Csepel
bike.[31]

He raked half-heartedly enough, but in the end he had something
to show for it. An old friend of his was passing by. He noticed
right away but did not stop working until the last moment. The
man had grown fat. Also, they did not like each other very much
in the past, at least he didn't, but this had no meaning under the
circumstances. They started a pleasant conversation. While they
were chatting, at least he didn't have to rake.

There was talk of the young man's family, his mother-in-law,
always lying, intriguing, the factory; then out of the blue he was
going to leave 'this bawdy house' within a year, he said. At first
he didn't catch on. The blond young man said he was leaving
the country, 'a toolmaker can make a living anywhere, old man,
even in Canada'.

'Here, too,' (. . . .) said simply but logically. 'You tell me how
long I am supposed to put up with my fucking mother-in-law!'
'But really,' he started to say, then could not finish. 'I see,' he
said instead, leaning on the rake. He thought it preposterous,
funny and horrible, outrageous, sad and deeply tragic, shameful
and *da capo* hilarious that of all days he was cleaning the front

---

[31] Csepel bike: a Trabant on two wheels (*cf., Notes by the author*).

of his humble abode for the 4th of April, Liberation Day, so the house wouldn't be the object of talk.

A matter of form

Watching a political rally on television, he recalled what Wittgenstein had once read in *Simplicissimus*. Two professors are listening to the shouts of the men working on the construction of a bridge with a complex structure; *obi, aufi, dran*, since all this was in German, of course. They are amazed. 'It is a mystery, dear Colleague, how work requiring such care and precision can be done in this language.'

He had read that former American Secretary of State Haig was pilloried by the *local* watchmen of the language; sentence structure, diction, inflection and the like; and it would do him good, the experts advised, if he'd speak nothing but Latin for a couple of months. He fantasised with glee about the comrades from Party Headquarters going to the Piarists (Father Treasure) for tutoring, *ego, sum*, et cetera.

The death of the master

He was having tea at the old Asztória Caré, picking at a plate of strawberries and whipped cream. The whipped cream had gone off, and he imagined it being sprayed on top of the strawberries from a fire extinguisher. Hamvas had written about strawberries, he remembered.

He saw a man throw a hand grenade from the balcony, glance detached after it, gulp down his coffee, and amidst the general confusion, walk out. He decided to follow. Two dead, and a little girl had lost her hand from the wrist down. One of the victims was a suntanned woman of about forty, a fine, elegant lady. (When he glanced inside the back of her low-cut dress, he saw her brassiere was held together by a rusty safety pin. How could that be?) The other victim was a man, his face disfigured by eczema.

He followed the man down Lajos Kossuth Street, then turned into Semmelweis Street. In front of the Spotted Lion by the Russian House of Culture, the man spun round and gave him a look, whereupon he also spun round and walked away. He was barely twenty-five at the time.

The punctuality of the east-european
'My business is Eastern Europe. This presumptuous statement is equivalent to a fish, prisoner of a battered, rust-stained bathrub, condemned to silence except for Christmas Eve, saying, my business is bathtubs. Besides, the filth surrounding us hasn't even got an intimate, domestic character; the water is ice cold, and we have to dodge life-size warships all the time.

'People around these parts are vigilant, hungry for knowledge. In those few precious moments when they are not forced to practise the switch-over to breathing through the gills, are not herded together by the bright beams of glaring ideologies, when their peace is not shattered by the blast of hand grenades, they come out of the water, look around and, panting with the full weight of their many duties, attempt to come to grips with the lesson to be learned from swimming around the tub in circles. What are we to do? What must a man do in order not to take the bait? What can and what must literature do under the circumstances?

'Just one thing, and without balking. It must provide a clear description of the situation. It must make a proper assessment. This clear-headed precision is not much, but it is not little either. It is not much if we think of how many have already declared our bathtub a free ocean, how many have re-enamelled it, carved, hammered, kneaded, forced, rapped and tapped it into shape, trying in this manner to talk us out of looking for the drainpipe; and it is not little if we consider how the seaweed of bias and prejudice has engulfed even this small body of water, how little we know even our own brood.

'Our work is cut out for us. We must put an end to the big words coming from the loudspeakers, the glaring lies which no one ever took seriously except us, and with clear and sober minds we must come to recognise the situation for what it is, and learn to accept ourselves and Eastern Europe, too. We must become Eastern Europeans so we may become Europeans – and once, perhaps, even proper human beings,' he read from Endre Bojtár.

They

He watched his friend work. He hadn't shaved in days. His face was dark like a tombstone. He was worried about him. He sat and watched his friend making a kitchen cabinet.

'Because, what is it I am really doing,' his friend muttered. (. . . .) considered that all manner of expert handiwork was like consorting with the devil. Before he had grown to hate them, he had an inordinate respect for craftsmen. His friend was a whiz at joining the pieces together. 'I am fencing in space'. (. . . .) nodded. He was fencing it in, no two ways about it. 'And why? So I can put a glass in it. Which is what? The fencing in of space. I could have been a carpenter once. But now . . . how can anyone be *serious* about a profession such as this? A fencing-inner of space . . .'

His friend liked to think seriously about things. He was like (. . . .)'s better self. (Our better self is no better than our other selves, of course, not even more *aspiring*. But it has a kind of seriousness, weighty and strong and orderly, which, though we are loath to admit, we think very highly of. Except, of course, when we are talking about ourselves.)

This friend of his is a novelist with four children, two of whom he, it is a shame but there you have it! nearly despises (the way they gorge down their food, and laugh, and play, screaming or quietly, it's disgusting), and recently his wife left him, too. She's left. She's not there.

He sat in the kitchen like a bad *kibitz*. He had a mounting headache, and his friend's hammering was becoming excruciating, barely tolerable.

And so, the question comes up: *what is space?* Is it really something from which you can *fence a bit off*?

Theatre

He received a letter with a yellow paper daisy glued to the back. Someone had written on it: REVISED BY SARAH. Sarah was the wife of the man who had written the letter. He thought it highly sensuous, as if the flower had been pasted on the envelope behind the husband's back, in secret and in face of a thousand dangers, like a good drawing-room comedy. Beyond the fence

strewn with oyster shells stood a number of blackened tombstones. As he glanced out at the ocean glittering pale and distant
beyond the tombstones, he suddenly felt profound scorn for the
woman's husband, a man who would not capture his wife's heart,
he read.

The laughter of the gods

He was often bothered, especially when reading so-called descriptions, about how the corner of a mouth drooped here and a sense
of melancholy perched on an earlobe there, which made him
think of people as if they were animals. But his embarrassment
was not genuine.

A woman

A woman called him, suggesting they meet. She said what an
awful lot it would mean to her, and so on. He lived alone and
was more courteous than humane with the woman, who was
using expressions that frightened him, saying he 'should take
pity on her', he should 'at least give her a chance', and he
'shouldn't do this to her'. Meanwhile the line went dead several
times, and a symphony orchestra was rehearsing in the background. This bothered the woman very much, and it was plainly
ridiculous. As he listened to her full admission, his fingers insol-
ently playing with the receiver, he had the pleasant sensation that
he was mortifying her.

'You're a coward and a prick,' said Sulamith of the ashen hair,
the stranger with the lovely name. This happened seven years
ago.

The expert
One: everything is mercy. Two: love me. The man who said this said it as if a sophisticated cosmic sergeant were parrying a thrust, *un, deux* . . .

His family
His stomach rumbled. The man he was sitting with had an ancestor who, to put it bluntly, was Haydn's employer. With an eye to this fact the progeny said, see, as for me, I have to make do with the *music-making* of my stomach. Whereupon he said it's only democratic. He sounded as offended as a Workers Union representative.

The innkeeper's diary
The social programme of the *Kurfürst*: 'Learn to be afraid of your servants.'

Get the picture?
At one time, or so his family lore would have it, it was on the stomach of the elegant, refined and accomplished old lady who at times could be as selfish as a sparrow-hawk and whom he visited from time to time, sitting on the side of her beautiful bed, because the old lady did not like to get up any more, preferring to lounge on her bed in fabulous, dreamy nightgowns, her wrist and neck laden with jewels, they drank coffee and scotch whisky and nibbled dried prunes, which were the woman's *favourite titbit*, hurriedly, almost hastily dispensing with the inconsequential details of their private lives so they could turn to the affairs of the world, wider relationships which the lovely

matron, regardless of how they'd approach them, would always see in a more optimistic light than he, who, for his part, would always call her attention to a number of basic untruths and quoted the fact that a clear source could be muddied by the least amount of dirt, which the woman accepted, turning sad for a moment, which he also respected in her, this deep and fleeting sadness, but you must admit, my dear, that never before, *do you understand me?* never before did this country have it so good, just look around you (here he began to make a wry face in earnest, because you can always find a subset in which we are the king of the dunghill), and though it's obvious how you can't come out with the truth, *just like that*, but neither can you do it *in earnest* anywhere else, for that matter, besides, today you can say more than yesterday, and tomorrow more than today, don't you agree?; he listened with awe because at the time even what he disagreed with did not appear to him as the obligatory optimism of a certain type of political thinking, and if it did, this didn't bother him either, in all honesty, he conceived of it as peace of mind, feminine and wise, i.e., Time that doth watch over us all would find a way out in spite of us – in short, the gentlemen, meaning her future husband and his companions, were supposed to have played cards on her stomach.

Later on, when he sat on the edge of her bed, at the base of the jewels, drinking coffee and whisky and nibbling on the dried prunes, the gradual disappearance of which the old lady watched with a sidelong, apprehensive flutter, and listened to the progressive description of his homeland, desperate, he couldn't think of anything else except, WHAT A HAND! WHAT A RUN OF CARDS! (*I have written a progressive description of my country*, he mumbled as he re-read it so that later he could honestly say: this is not true.)

Dialogue
'Why are you criticising the social order?'

'Because I see all the bad this <*corrupt text*> regime has produced.'

'You do? I thought you did not admit to a difference between good and bad. How about the way *you* live?'

Thus did he converse with the angel, though truth to tell, this particular angel was wearing an impeccable top hat . . .

Old hat
When the organisation which served to guarantee the security of the citizens, but most especially of the state, had grown riot like bad weed and had decided that right up there with the counts, peasants, neo-Nazis, the United States of America, and *last but not least* the communists themselves the above-mentioned lady also posed a threat to the state, she was called in for a little chat. When they took down the records they asked for her date of birth. It was at night, and there they stood around her, a bunch of haggard and surly men, because it was night. 'You mustn't ask a *gentlewoman* her age, young man!'

When he continued to ply her, asking her what happened next, the old lady caressed the young man's face, who blushed and his heart began to race. She kept her withered yet remarkably light hand – he had never felt such lightness before in his life – on his cheek, the fingers reaching the folds of the forehead, and shrugged. 'What happened, my dear? I really can't recall.'

Rain

'How obvious I am,' he thought after he'd taken the spoon out of the coffee cup of the guest who'd just left without the least sign of aversion. It was raining at the time.

The murderer

A decadent youth, a straw between his lips, his delicate hand on his waspish waist, *helló evree-boddee!*, asked very meekly, really, 'Why are we making such a fuss over this freedom and truth business . . .?' He didn't answer. He thought instead, for the first time in ages, to be sure, that he should sleep with a cute girl he knew. Meanwhile, the young people left. At that moment he'd have given his life for that girl.

Night

Late at night, when the house is like a tomb whence no laughter issues, when only the thirty-two-year-old man was still puddling about as was his wont, a friend of his showed up. They talked till midnight over tea. At midnight he saw him outside. But trembling with cold, they continued talking on the corner till about two-thirty. On his way back, this time alone, he thought how nice it was the way it was, no high points and no intellectual ferment, perhaps his joy was so tangible because his friend rarely dropped by *just like that*, out of the blue.

At this point he felt a pang of conscience. Maybe *something was wrong*, and that's why his friend had visited him, it's just that they never got around to it? He made a face. He was cold, but did not go inside. He reviewed the evening, searching for clues . . . Possibly when his friend said that about life being *so little*, could there be no more to it than teaching, passing it on? which he realised now he'd misunderstood, saying how a life of action is equally puny, it's all round him, not that it's puny for *him*, of course, but it is for those who live a life of action. Rather clever of me, he murmured in the dark. He could not decide if anything was wrong or not.

A hard night descended upon him. In a sky chiselled smooth by the wind, like a pane of Formica, the stars showed like silver flakes, tarnished now and again by the yellow gleam of a revolving light. Perfumes of spice and warm stone were wafted on the breeze. A couple of streets down a car must have skidded on the wet pavement, then silently drove away, and in its wake distant, confused cries rent the air. Then, like a dense veil slowly falling from the starry sky, silence returned. His friend was an atheist, but he lived as if he were a God-fearing man. Only his humility and asceticism seemed a bit too obvious, a consequence, surely, of his struggle with pride rooted in real values.

The age

From an upstairs window he glanced down on the narrow street. A sudden silence descended on the city. A lean young man hurried softly in the wake of another, *I love you*, he heard upstairs, like a prayer (prayerette) among the grey, dusty, thin branches. Blood-red Trabants sped past – a mortal two-stroke rhythm.

Tokyo

There was a much published, inordinately active and ideologically assertive man, immoderately so, whose name out of a combination of cowardice and well-considered self-interest he will not divulge.

Anyway, when he had caught him yet again doing something he considered plain treacherous, to say the least, he came up with the following ornate epithet: HE IS A NEWSPAPERMAN DESERVEDLY BELOVED FROM SOVIET MOSCOW TO THE BULGARIAN SOFIA, FROM THE SALTY WARNE-MÜNDE TO THE SWEET ROMANIAN MAMAIA. But once he was finished, he felt a tinge of sadness. How *could* he have found the time for such utter nonsense?

Death

He has a friend he'd never met in person, and he often thinks that perhaps he never will. This is one of the pleasant little secrets of his life. His mother died. On the day of the funeral, his friend unexpectedly called him. Up till then they had only corresponded by mail. 'I heard,' he said. It is all he said. Then he began to cry. He had called several times since, but without saying a word. He just cries into the phone. This crying is their friendship.

Colour effect

He was enjoying the company of friends. This company of friends, however, did not consist only of his friends; it was too much fun for that, more intense, more joyful. You need a friend or two, of course, just so they can put the *kibosh* on the merriment, which in the end they don't, and though the company of friends would remain a company of friends without them, we, on the other hand, would then *not be there*.

Later they found themselves out on the street, where a cold wind was howling; they walked arm in arm, veritably swept along by the wind, their white scarves flapping, silver balls of saliva on the rough knit, a handsome youth, ponytail, rouge, the giggling of adolescent girls, cement square, silk, a pair of ice-cold eye-glasses, strange cement dust, colour effect.

Then suddenly – a bad joke – they heard a loud rumble. He was startled out of his early-morning stroll like some preposterous cartoon character, grabbing the first available woman (so to speak), flinging his arms tight around her. 'I'm scared. Hug me.' They had a good laugh over that. Later one of the adolescent girls by the name of Jitka secretly stroked his back, the way they do the flanks of light-coloured soda-wagon horses. 'It's all right.'

At a later point, when he had a chance to press his head to the belly of a woman, more or less a stranger to him, he was inordinately grateful to Heaven for the way things stood.

Handcuffs
When the erudite gentleman and the scandal monger who'd come up with the phrase, 'our Party caucus leaves us in the raucous', saw the bunch of carnations he was taking to a woman, he asked, 'Taking it for a walk?' For days he thought this was highly amusing.

Moon
They were sitting among the dark rocks in the depth of the garden, in leafy bowers and celestial abysses. But the conversation was light. Basically, they agreed that art had never been the idyllic isle of bliss that could withstand the whirling, foaming, filthy tide of life, a place where one could lean back and read

Pascal. Conversely, it springs from this filthy tide, and it is from *there*, and it is *this* which rises towards God, if only for a brief instant, or even towards ourselves, for man is holy, too, and is more than the sum of all the sorry parts we get to see of ourselves. That was the drift of their conversation.

Then a moonbeam abruptly illuminated his guest's face, and the face seemed so foreign, so strange, he felt he didn't know who was sitting across from him; he didn't even know *where they were*. The trees stirred, and with his head lowered he thought, what's the difference, *something's* got to give.

Playing with fire

He felt weightless, as if he had no conscience, even, just raw nerves. As if he didn't even exist . . .. When they got in the car, the woman threw him a look and said, 'Won't you be sorry?' 'No.' His answer was sincere. The woman pressed his hand and said, *I* won't be sorry either, but . . .' Her face looked once again as if illuminated by the light of the moon.

The pillow

He dreamt that somebody was telling him how he'd seen the parson kick his assistant Ferkó in the ass, shouting and cackling in the meantime, 'There's the Order of the Ass for you, there's the great big Order of the Ass for you!' Then the person telling the story shrugged – a slapdash rite! – and said, 'But what has that got to do with the Office for Church Affairs? ' He didn't know, not in his dream, nor in the morning, as he stretched long and pleasurably, like a cat . . .

Spartan discipline

He received a call from the radio inviting him for an unbridled chat. When he understood at last what they wanted – *hauptmotif*: democracy – he drew a deep breath (later uneasily thinking it could be heard over the phone); thank you but no thank you, he can't chat *unbridled*, in this country he can't chat unbridled regardless of how tame and pleasant he might be by nature (he is well brought up and open-hearted otherwise, except he's running out of otherwises); *bridled* is the only way he could talk, and that's something he hates, so as long as he's got a say, he makes sure not to get into situations like that.

The sympathetic female voice said she understood, she knew what (. . . .) must be feeling, and she respected his feelings, and she wouldn't want to by pushy, but this could be something good, honest, a brand-new series, she was able to get some very good human *material*, and her boss backs her, too. It promises to be worth while. 'Is that a fact?' 'Perhaps,' continued the female voice rather timidly, 'this bridled-unbridled thing shouldn't be taken quite so seriously . . .' 'See? That's just it,' he cried into the phone merrily, 'that's just the point!'

Exhaustion

The doe-eyed man, handsome, brown-haired, with impressive serratus magnus muscles, had said to him, 'Don't be so *exclusive*.' This made him reflect. He even felt a little bit ashamed. *He got off easy with just that exclusive!* But then he went and did precisely what the brown-haired man had called exclusive.

Revenge

It was already the second time he had to cross Lenin's name out of the text. One reference was no doubt frivolous, just plain frivolous, while the other was innocent in every way. May my hand shrivel off if ever I write his name again, he said in his heart of hearts, unjustly *vis à vis* the leader of the working-class movement, who clearly couldn't be faulted with all this. He was annoyed that he had gotten so entangled in this thing, but had no idea how he could have done it differently. If it were Pascal, at least . . . Oh, Ilich! What a lot of nonsense.

Consolidation

Watchword: They never stop at a pleasant droning and humming. Sometimes they *give it to you straight*. They gave it to him *straight*, too, telling him not to use the <*self-censored*> sign so much. Because sometimes when he thought something could not stand print, or others thought so, but he wanted to give a sign of his cowardice nevertheless or, to put it less pridefully, a hint of his lack of consistency and good taste, this was how he signified the intellectual and societal act of self-censorship. Since the reasoning of those who were *giving it to him* was highly cogent and attractive, he began leaving the said sign out, putting in instead what he had left out – provided there was anything.[32] And that's how he was published.

The thing can be further complicated if we start off with the word 'self-censored'. We get the message, we cross it out, but since we are not rascals, we indicate the fact, we put in <*self-*

[32] Stylisation has grown to such proportions that we treat metaphors as if they were 'the thing itself'. Thus are we losing our good sense, you and me, both.

censored>; they give it to us, we feel intimidated, we acquiesce, so we cross <*self-censored*> out and put back: self-censored. As you can see, the text is hardly changed (long live close attention to detail!), while the poor domestic pen-pusher feels less than triumphant. And so does the reader. And if you don't know why, think of the fact that what has been said above might have also been influenced by what has been said above . . .

So far so good. Gutsy. Progressive. Managed to put something into words again. Except, there's me to contend with again. It's me castrating myself (and that's an exaggeration, though I haven't said half!). Of course, when in a squeaky little voice I yell *shark! shark!*, that ain't nothin' neither, even if the sharks are not easily scared. It's not their job. Still, some of the sunbathers on the narrow strip of beach will raise their heads and, alarmed, call their little critters to them, or let their hands drop on their muscular companions' stomachs, or sit up grinning, enjoying the wild dance of the sharks.

However, let us face facts. The squeaky little voice is absurd. And this fact is in no wise mitigated by the colourful spectacle of our two bloody balls bobbing up and down and away on the murky ocean waves . . . Fine. I know. Life is not a bowl of cherries. We wobble our way out of the water, the sand is lovely and hot, and we place our hands under our heads. We've got the sky in the mornin' and the moon at night. Worse comes to worse, we stop daydreaming about the other sex. We lay a fluffy bath towel on our groins, and with lowered eyes, elated and terrified, we think about our lives.

176

The helping verbs of the heart

He loved the woman, his 'old friend', very much. What that
meant he did not bother his head about; but whenever he thought
of her he also thought he loved her. Once he asked her anyway,
'Do you love me?' The woman nodded. 'Which makes you my
lover,' (. . . .) said. The woman shook her head. 'I am not,' and
here she held a long and ugly pause, 'literature.' And they left it
at that.

At other times they'd walk, except such a sharp wind would
arise, they'd clench their teeth, which disfigured their faces. This
put them in a foul mood. However, this is not entirely true; their
mood was indistinct. But it was nevertheless chilly.

This happened on a burning February morning when his mother,
Beatríz Viterbo, died, after braving an agony that never for a
single moment gave way to self-pity or fear; and he noticed that
a sidewalk billboard on Vörösmarty Square was advertising some
new brand or other of cigarettes. The fact pained him, for he
realised that the wide and endless universe was already slipping
away from her and that this slight change was the first of an
endless series of changes.

Marriage

His girlfriend is a knock-out with long, tumbling locks and what
have you. She started ageing a while back, but then stopped,
because she fell in love with her husband again. The phone
clicked mysteriously, distant noises came through the receiver, as
if some material were trickling through the wire. This diverted
his attention. Then he heard, 'I am not cut out to be an artist's
wife.' He laughed. 'I'm sorry, madame, but that's ridiculous.' No

answer, just the distant noise. Then he added, 'But most ridiculous of all is the word artist.'

Homework
Underline all facts pertaining to the anti-revolutionary character of the events of 1956.[33] (From the eighth-grade history book.) Just watch all the little schmucks underline!

Vox humana
Possibly the greatest crime of this regime, our regime, is that it has banished the human voice from all areas of our lives.

The gourmet
The restaurant was known for its fine cuisine, though the food was nothing special, considering. Humdrum. But like the hero of a Krudy novelette, in the end he ordered 'a light soup'. His friend was in trouble, that was the topic of their conversation. In the adjacent booth there sat a corpulent man with a woman who brought just one word to mind: unappetising. His friend sent a hearty greeting their way. Then, talking into his beard with a strange, annoying circumspection which reminded him of an histrionic aside, he proceeded to say that this was the man who had attempted to 'brush him off the map' right after their graduation. He made the appropriate gesture, whereupon the waiter rushed over, apologised, and with a snow-white kerchief swept the table clean. Just like a barber in a farce.

[33] 1956: just like the previous freedom fights. Although it produces some impressive partial results, it etc., etc., etc.

(. . . .) felt a surge of gratitude. 'Thank you.'

An introduction to literature
What a feeling to watch our own separate world (version: the world) as it gradually rounds out like a beautiful rubber ball right before our eyes! 'I can learn almost nothing without the new knowledge finding its well-appointed place in some corner of the old,' Nietzsche writes. The proof is in the pudding.

Fragments
Sit on my lap and *inspire* me! Dingle my dangle, *I wanna see things from a brand-new angle!* . . . Oh, miss, you are risking your reputation on my pointed re*cap*-itulation.

He hears 'ostracism', he says (slowly, a mistake) the house where you 'suffered criticism'.

'You are terrorising me and you think it's all right because you are terrorising yourself as well.'

Hemingway is a writer, somebody said, and Proust is not a writer, because Hemingway knows what it is to catch fish. This surprised him. Why is it more *substantial* to know how to catch fish than to understand the nature of a *kiss on the hand*?!

There's a woman with auburn hair and a big nose. Sometimes she is ugly, sometimes she is beautiful and radiant. He can't take his eyes off her.

A cunt-violin, said the mason about the bidet, and winked.

He writes: 'A boy is sleeping in the stable on the rotting straw. Two women peep in, the princess and the camp follower. "Let's mount him. Get yourself hoist on his petard." The boy is frightened.'

He finds it almost unbearable when his ballpoint pen makes a scratching sound.

He turns in supplication to the actor playing the spy. 'Look here, handsome. Please. An Alain Delon inside a *Michel* Farkas. Get it?'

His uncle died, the one who in the course of a game once came up with *hactus* for the letter 'h'. Easy-go-lucky adolescents that they were, they accepted it. Ever since, *hactus* is something we have to contend with.

'My fiancé teaches solmisation in Baghdad,' said a girl with the simplicity reserved for the rain when it is really raining. He loved her for it. On the other hand, he also had to laugh at her. Solmisation? In Baghdad?

All night he stares at a ▼, the mystery of the moss.

Cranach's trees are the trees of the universe, says the poet Pilinszky. This had never occurred to him.

Et cetera. Otherwise, I'm in fine spirits, possibly a bit under the weather; sometimes amusing, at other times annoying things happen to me, but the clockwork is up to par, tick-tock, tick-tock, even if a fly should happen to alight on it or a nightingale should be heard to sing in the garden . . .

Con-tempo ...

He received a letter from <*self-censored*>. 'My dear friend! As you might have guessed from the time that has since elapsed, I have agonised much over our previous plan for a solution, but in the end I thought it best not to play havoc with your powerful, poetic text with its barbaric parenthetical comments. Without them it would lose its pith and marrow, its sensational aspect. But the prohibitions are still standing, especially here. I suggest another journal or possibly inclusion in a book, or else that we *mutually wait it out.* After all, more important than any present publication is the fact that you have put pen to paper. Best regards ...'

Giving free rein to his natural reflexes he first blew his top, sweeping up and down the room like a whirlwind, the dust *ringing* at his heels. Well I'll be! The nerve! Humph! Huh! And: up yours, friend! (So far so good; being mortally wounded in his pride, he could at least have resort to dignity as an alibi. Wounded-pride crop-rotation.) He was used to their methods of course, which, frankly, especially as far as he was concerned, weren't even very glaring, just so ... so very *primitive*!

That such a shamefully staged give and take should take seven months, only to be topped off by this ridiculous letter, well and good. But that in the meantime they should *regularly* not speak to him, that was going over the top. (There were criminally few places he could recall where he *should* have entered with respect but could not, György Rónay, he was the exception. He sat in the waiting room with butterflies in his stomach, the snow melting from his shoes, and he trying to hide them. 'Why are you making such a mess, boy,' Rónay asked. He often remembered that; why indeed is he making such a *mess*? Rónay, as the joke

would have it, had seen Lenin, what I mean is, the poet
Babits . . .)

'Time elapsed', 'pith and marrow', he rolled these epistolary
masterpieces on his tongue, yes, and the prohibitions as they
stand, this he imagined right off, visually, him leaning against
the penis-prohibitions, Parliament engirded by the gallant prohibitions, their cute little blue-and-red heads proudly reaching
for the sky, face right! present arms!, then the same prohibitions
as withered old mammies begging at the base of the First House
of the Nation . . . He was also much impressed by the depth and
scope, to wit, what's the big deal over one silly publication, our
mutual baseness, when we should be rejoicing, pith and marrow
and sensation, it's a veritable holiday, 'you have put pen to paper'!
May the pox take him, and so on and so forth!

He wanted to include it somewhere at all cost, he was even
ready to compromise, braced for a bit of East-European drop in
standards. Let the supposed precision of the text perish as long
as it is *included*. There was a place, for instance, his place, where
they had 'blasted into the bawdy house', you should've seen prose
scram and the objects fly through the air, bricks crashing, 4 in.
partition walls, plaster chips, cross-beams, rafters, lashings and
liners, purlin, window frames, door knobs, the pleasure-loving
stonemason Sándor Csibi, Sándor Sebök, his assistant with the
wooden leg, tiles, a picture frame, a Csontváry reproduction, a
black bra, a man's hat with nosegay, a pair of dentures, the
Hungarology Bulletin, a walking stick, condom, top hat, a yellow
Chandler volume, garters, another bra, purple, a book of essays
by Thomas Mann, the score of *Hommage à Dohnányi*, panties,
very dirty and in very many ways, small suppositories, full discre-
tion. First the girls: their chests expanded, their breasts naked,

the nipples of their bosoms rending the air suffused with brick-powder, but one is laughing, though some are crying, while some faces are obstinately off limits. The men clasp their hands in front of their privates, their undershirts immaculate as they hurl themselves into the deep.

So then. He imagined the letter with the conspicuous letter-head of the journal in question, out of a pair of blood-battered fur panties – and that's that. But as he *tasted* the scene trippingly on the tongue, the attention that was being paid to detail in higher quarters put a fly in his ointment. The same thing happened two more times. He was on the verge of taking this for a celestial sign, and he thought he would have to kiss his simple, legitimate, and just barely primitive literary revenge goodbye. But in the end, when he had resigned himself and with a grand gesture had yielded in his heart, success came knocking at the door.[34] 'There's got to be *some* risk in being editor-in-chief. And in the fact that there are some things you can do, and some you cannot,' he grumbled.

Life

'S. was in love with my mother but had to make do with my father.'

Wings

'His self-control is not callousness, his callousness is not a sign of disinterest, his disinterest is not a sign of something *lacking*,' he wrote. 'A certain *lack* is unavoidable. We have little (if any)

[34] Daily programme: looking the truth straight between the eyes. (Babits)

alternative.' The editor crossed out the last part of the sentence and when he asked why, he was told to stop being a wise guy, what does he mean we have little if any alternative, why this *ex officio* pessimism, why must he make such a drastic statement in this *economico-politico-culturalico situation*; he will go a step further, in fact, it is plain irresponsible, words and actions must stay rooted in reality, and said reality is not the sky with fleecy clouds, he should give the emperor his due, and *then* we'll see what's what with his god, 'provided he exists', not that he wants to make an issue out of it, it can be the other way around for all he cares, as long as people stop this false historical squealing, 'what the horse's balls do they want, you can't make America in thirty years, not with a past like this, we have the Turk to contend with, the primitive accumulation of capital is child's play in comparison, *for God's sake.*' Besides, there's freedom of religion. And he patted him on the back: 'Don't go looking for shit, it'll hit the fan of its own accord.'

He couldn't care less, he said slyly when he went to the editor-in-chief to tell (!) on the editor,[35] he wrote a couple of sentences about a novelist, so what, what's the fuss, he's not running down the government *exactly*, though given half a chance he wouldn't hold himself in check, there's no government or party these days you couldn't run down from morning to night, workers of the world unite!, why should ours be any different; not that he wants to pretend (that would entail lying!) that around these parts *it's the way*, no, it's not the way, in the upper and semi-upper echelons they like to lean back at such times, like frail old countesses, *my dear, the smelling salts!*, and besides – and may the name of Party

[35] A fine example of the East-European multi-party system.

Headquarters be blessed – the consumption of smelling salts is diminishing, and that's something at any rate, seeing how it's imported from Austria, for *hard* currency . . .

'Look. Don't gab so much,' the editor-in-chief said. He seemed uninterested. Then he waved an arm (two arms), nonsense, of course he can keep that half-sentence, why does *he* have to *push* everything *through himself.* And he's expected to make democracy with subordinates like these? How much blood, sweat and tears it takes to make people live with the rights which, for chrissakes, are theirs!; as for the sentence, he doesn't think it's *fortunate*, it *breaks the curve*, but if (. . . .) insists, leave it, it's his article, after all, just cross out the parenthetical *if any*, 'it's another one of your uncalled-for mannerisms, friend'. And he patted him on the back.

This patting on the back must have been the cement that kept the editorial staff together. It must have been the *kernel* of their principles, the *root* of consensus.

Mirrors

'The object of criticism *draws strength* from criticism. It gives the stamp of approval with its name even when it is saying, *I will not give it the stamp of approval with my name!*' 'Pure sophistry.' 'No. You've got to be aware. But not use it as an alibi, as if it made no difference. *It makes a difference.*' ('The reason we're keeping you and your friends on,' a well-known potentate was supposed to have said as he dipped the tip of his tongue into the home-made pálinka, 'is to say things that are risqué. And now you've turned *loyalists* on us?')

Playing with fire

'I can't pray,' the friend he had lunch with the other day told him, his voice grainy with desperation. 'Understand? I cannot pray.' 'Yes,' he said. 'Let me.' For a second this frightened him. Then after he'd put the phone down, furtively like an illegal street peddler, he launched into prayer.

A painter

He was strolling with the painter *in the light of day*. A rare happenstance. He was saying how before he'd take a picture of everything, 'what do you mean *everything?*' the other asked, whereupon the painter began to nod enthusiastically, 'yes, that's just it, every single *thing*, the universe,' that's why he stopped taking pictures, he felt he shouldn't be so *generous* with his *presence*.

One shabbily bright shop window followed the next, and always he discovered something. One of the shop windows was boarded up. He peeked through a gap in the boards. He saw a mattress in the middle of the deserted, decrepit store, a rust-stained, large, awkward, clapped-out affair, on it a woman, writhing and twisting as if this were a peep show. He did not tell the painter, but wondering, resumed his walk. It was pink between the woman's legs, like a piglet's. In the light of day, in the light of day!

A woman

He'd been living with a woman for seven years. He loved her very much. One morning he found himself *drinking in the sight of her.* It hurt him physically that he had to leave, but he had to leave.

If a man ...
If a man's got a Trabant, he feels about the Trabant the way he feels about the government.

We have driven out the aristocrats, what a comforting thought, the land divided up, the factory ours, *I will not give back the land!*, all of which is super-duper, there's no praise that'll do it justice. And still. One's up here with this whole rigmarole.

We don't have to go on foot. Fine. We don't have to take the bus. Fine. Except, suddenly we're up to our ears with this two-stroke inanity. Being the owner of a Trabant (made in GDR) is *more desirable* than what we've got around us in one respect only, namely, that there is a thoroughly *comforting* alternative at least – a *Diesel Golf.*

Nota bene: need we add, it is *all* fuelled by the corrective impulse of I'm angry *with* you, not *against* you. – In the *corrective* meaning of the term, *of course.*

A prisoner
As he walked along the street with possibly more haste than was absolutely called for, thereby standing out from the crowd of idle strollers, he thought how little he liked it when someone approached him on the sidewalk with a happy I'm-on-cloud-nine-look, someone with a smile on his lips. What nerve! Disgusting! And the thought made him smile.

Death

There was quite a crowd gathered around on the nearby corner. He approached cautiously, as if sneaking up on some animal he did not wish to frighten away. A spider, for instance. A young man on a motorbike had skidded, it must have just happened, they were lifting the motorbike off his leg, it's all he could see, his leg, his bloodsoaked jeans torn at the thigh. *Dusty blood.* In the back row in front of him he heard two men engaged in a whispered exchange. They were the same sort – their tapered shirts and fine, light shoes, for one. What he heard was, 'I love her. Though that's not the right expression. She is a part of me. Don't think I hate you or harbour any ill feelings. No. *You do not count.*'

He fought his way to the front. A girl with short hair dyed red was sitting on the curb, swinging her helmet back and forth, her face like a deserted landscape. The steering wheel of the motorbike stuck out of the boy's neck like a butcher's knife. He wore the same checked shirt she did. He grabbed on to his own. A policeman was approaching. He looked as worn out as a stonemason.

Olga

'Olga!' he yelled. 'That white-livered predator!' his friend added. 'Don't be silly . . .' They went to a joint that called itself a café, where they agreed that the morose waitress had a face like dear old Chekhov's wife. Just then a couple asked if they could sit at their table, and their conversation ground to a halt.

The corpse

A woman across the way was standing on top of a table, adjusting the red sunshade. The wind swept up the volunteer parachute and, with a scream, the woman fell several storeys. He glanced down. He saw the corpse, white, arms and legs splayed, almost a perfect X-shape. From the apartment, the husband did not see or hear anything. He could see on his face the annoyed impatience brought on by the sunshade which was still not in its place.

Life and death

'Oh, my Grey Brother the Wolf, may peace be with you and your people. My leg is broken, alas, and my pain, as you can see, is great instead of small. Oh, death of deaths . . .' Biting his pen, he came forward. 'Go back, go back,' the little girl screamed. 'Never scream like that *before it is time*, sugar . . .' 'Help, help, oh, my brother the grey wolf!' 'Shush. To wait patiently for the man with the red hair to steal out of his lair is what I advise. For all you know, his intentions may be honourable. Believe me, you'd be better off.'

His brother's children were bored with his talk but were scared to do anything else. He watched them with distaste. 'All I wanted to say is do not *play* with death so much. Do not shout, oh, I die, I die, but hurray, I live, help me, my dear friend. DO YOU UNDERSTAND?!' Head bowed, he walked back to his desk.

The same day

He got on a bus. The schoolgirl on the seat in front of him was whispering something to a boy. It was in French. The boy's nape was lovely, downy and delicate, like a doe in the reeds. Two old women were giggling, oh, that Louis XVth, Lou, got himself a pig in a poke, a Jèselska, or what's her name.' 'You don't say! A pig in a poke?!' They giggled, abashed, and talked of the king as if he were the neighbourhood greengrocer who, though he has nice produce, cheats you from time to time.

That day everything made him happy. But in the evening he thought he may have been rather too superficial.

Pictures at an exhibition

It was raining and he felt the dampness in his bones. Outside in the hall a man in a fake fur coat was nervously walking up and down. They gazed suspiciously at each other. 'He's waiting for a woman, no doubt.' When he rang, an elderly lady opened the door. She said her daughter was not at home, then showed him the apartment. It was a kind of domestic exhibition with so-called modern pictures. The lady puttered in his wake, but without being obtrusive. She was not too objective, but she was not entirely uninformed either. He liked most of the pictures. They shook hands at parting, which made him think of the young women of the twenties with bobbed hair, the ones he liked so much. The man was still shuffling about in the hall. 'The woman's giving him the run-around.' Outside in the drizzle he remembered the woman's face, her characteristic and rather large nose, the bright and intelligent eyes. 'Good.'

The great earthquake

He joined the poet at his table. The poet was eating peasant-style smoked ham with his son, a big and awkward lad. They would sometimes *feed* each other, and this was so *sweet*. Hardly waiting to swallow his food, the poet plunged into some fantastic and obscure story about '56, the stormy give and take of threats and promises, 'after the dead the grass grows different'. (Concretely, that we should meet behind the statue of a great Hungarian, somebody said, but I'm warning you, don't go to such and such a spot this afternoon, somebody else said, or you'll regret it for the rest of your life. And that same night, somebody else, with a gun in his hand! 'You?!' 'What, did you expect, old man?!' 'Don't you be so familiar with me.')

The daily mail

He received an anonymous letter. It was signed, actually, but that was just a joke. The letter was so thoroughly devoid of any kind of threat, it was so lacking in direction, was so whimsical, in fact, it frightened him to death. Head bowed, he walked back to his desk.

Luck

The engineer of the soul cannot resort to the use of *policy*, he reflected. It is the difference between him and a city council president. He's got to be free, not useful. Which in practice means not loyal, but truthful . . . But what is truthful can be loyal – provided the gentlemen are lucky, isn't that right, gentlemen?

The madman's daughter

Once a poet and he were watching the 'new, vigorous young heifers' at the swimming pool – it was their training time! – and this reminded the poet of a story, namely, that once in his youth, when he had done what was expected of him like a *real man*, panting, sweating and satisfied he turned on his side and reached for a cigarette when the girl grabbed him by the shoulder and said right into his mug, 'Listen, you! Couldn't you have held that guck back for another two hours?'

The story almost made him puke. They watched the girls, the young calves, with two minds. They seemed innocent enough. (*P.S.* After thinking about it for a week, he asked the poet, 'Are you sure she said two hours?' 'Yes.' Plus: 'I should have known by the set of her chin she'd gobble me up, that she was going to gobble me up . . .')

Butterfly

The congenial singer was saying how the prose-writers that were present – because there were several prose-writers in attendance – should take note. There is a *young and hungry crowd* out there that something should be done about, a *culture-vacuum*. He's not smart, all he can do is sing, which means he can't *talk* to them, but the writers should. A woman with a pointed behind called out, 'People are not afraid of singing. They're afraid of words.'

The woman later grabbed one of the newspapermen by the ear and presented her theory that a singer is always a man-woman, that's why women like them. 'When you men-men get to reach women, that will change the world.' 'Good,' he thought desperately, then sneaked out to the toilet.

Music
He would soon be able to hear the musical instrument behind the music, he reflected, the object, the object which produces the sound, *there*, that *thing* in Beethoven is not the Heavens, nor the Universe, nor God, but the kettledrums and the absence of the kettledrums. And that will be good.

As string quartet is good when they are no longer talking to each other. 'Who?' he asked coldly.

I saw B's dick, the famous pianist said simply if not on the occasion, still, during B-year. (Baby photo: Bartók Archives)

Bragging: I can hardly tell Cage from Mozart.

Mehr Licht!
Byron sent Goethe a message: *Mehr shit!* – more shit! Johann Wolfgang, who spent the rest of his days wondering about this (among other things), at the last moment of his life said, *Mehr nicht!* – no more! If I were German, he thought ingeniously, I'd spend my whole life writing Goethe paraphrases!

The sentence
An Ottlik sentence does not tremble. It stands firm on its feet. Like a big boat or a big black bird, it almost imperceptibly *sways*.

The task

It is no easy task to live and not lose heart, he read in Nietzsche.

The daily mail

He received a letter from a reader. It was dated June 16th and came from the village where, after his family had been deported, he had spent his childhood. The writer's first name was the same as his mother's. This was *too much*! In this letter the writer, clearly highly intelligent, carried on about a whole lot of things. Furthermore, and this surprised him inordinately, she even said that upon reading one of his books she felt dirty, which she simply could not get herself to regard as a *catharsis*, and was hoping that he was not describing his own experiences, because what sort of a life would that be? Then she wrote down a cautionary tale for his instruction. It was as follows. Two porcupines on a cold winter's day crowded close together to save themselves from freezing by their mutual warmth. Soon, however, they felt each other's spines, and this drove them apart again. Whenever their need brought them more closely together, this – evil – intervened, until, thrown this way and that, they found a moderate distance from each other at which they could survive best. This surprised him. He thought his book was precisely about this, this awkward play with *distance*.

The discreet charm of liberty

Morning and night he was copying, as if he were engaged in prayer, Ottlik's *School on the Frontier* on a single sheet of white paper . . . When he started on the last page his heart began to pound as if it were in a cage, really, and wanted to jump out. He was overcome by trepidation. His hands were shaking and after every sentence he had to put his pen down. He was terrified by the thought that just before the finishing line he'd ruin it, three months' *work* down the drain. (He called it work because he was not *that* impressed with himself.) He even entertained the vague impression that maybe he shouldn't have plunged into it to begin with, stuck-up ass that he was, 'and now you'll be sorry, just you wait and see . . .' Point by point, he reviewed all the eventualities. But how he could ruin it *at all* he had no idea.

Why

A writer whose works he had read but whom he had not met personally before unexpectedly asked him for a favour, not too small, considering it meant getting up early, yet not too great either, since he'd be free by noon, whereupon he automatically said yes.

When he got back in the afternoon, he grumbled. Why did he help? What made him do it? Was he a sucker? He was. But that's not the point.

It was his vanity. Which made him blush with shame. A mistake, he later decided.

Wings

They frisked him thoroughly, 'No guns,' he said, attempting to make a joke, 'words are not guns.' When the officer reached his groin, he let out a passionate yelp. 'I want you, you wild thing, you!' he whispered loud and clear. The other glanced at him, sober to the end. 'The exit's over there.' When he stepped out of the booth, he was grinning. Later, when he looked around

him, he saw that everyone was just like him, with a grin stuck
on their faces . . .

Rivers

When the flooding of the rivers begins, he thumbs through the
papers, anxious to learn the water level that day, and if it is higher
than before, he is content. His joy is not diminished by the tides,
the collapsed huts, the flooded wheat fields and other human and
societal tragedies. No. He thinks more along these lines: 'What
a river, the Tisza. So *talented*!'

The cat

'By the time I was discharged, there it was, *Izolda had changed*.
But it was too late, because by then I was discharged.' This is
what the loquacious, weak-chested old man said as he mowed
the grass in the garden. He could have retired as a full colonel,
he went on, and then he wouldn't have to trouble himself with
all sorts of *grass*. 'Would you believe (?!), from '46 to '53 I served
in Domestic Affairs, but then Izolda's family, who, to be perfectly
honest, young man, couldn't *afford* a brother-in-law from the
ÁVÓ, made me get a discharge.' Once he had to take a political
from Solymár to the prison at 60 Andrássy Road, a dangerous
out-and-out scoundrel, 'innocent, of course, poor man'; he took
the man down to the basement, placed a matchstick on the
ground and shot it out of its place from 4 yards with a handgun!
Then he said, 'Remember what you just saw. You're a clever
man. But do not forget what you just saw. I'll shoot you wherever
you are because no matter how much you squirm, you'll always
be bigger than a matchstick.'

In parting, the old man pressed his hand gratefully for having indulged him, and said that in his opinion a man should be accepted for what he is. 'Especially,' he said awkwardly, 'since there isn't much choice.' 'Yes, indeed, just as you say, old man.' He had grown stubble, had guck in his eyes and smelled sour, and afterwards, after the raking, it turned out that he mowed, too, more than his share.

He had no dignity, and he was as flexible and tough as a scraggy cat which, with a screech, always lands on its feet.

The joke

From up close he watched a colleague of his trample somebody into the ground, then lean over him. 'You know why you got that?' Full of hope, the victim heaved himself up. It was only natural. After all, it is always comforting when baseness can be explained. 'Why?' '*Just because!*' Then his colleague helped him up.

'I did as Marx did with Hegel,' his colleague said, who was attending a compulsory Marxist-Leninist seminar. 'I stood him from his head on his feet, and vice versa.' Then when this colleague complained that because of his frequent absences he would probably he kicked out, he suggested that he should say he had a vision, that there is a God, that God exists. They had a good laugh over that.

Mercy

Another time, too, he thought there was nothing wrong. He gradually became immersed in the simple, classical story of the film, noticing the T-shaped tear at the bottom of the screen, now sewn together; at the so-called emotional climax he was on the verge of tears, then his deep emotion gave way to elation, a kind of reassuring empathy. On the screen the fate of the young man went from bad to worse, his fiery glance was that of the sacrifice, the Lamb, as a consequence of which, or so he felt, *their* fate was improving, a profane deliverance. The handsome face of the young actor seemed, with very little exaggeration, to guarantee our own safety. But just as a profound silence occurred in the middle of a heart-rending scene, then, in this silence conjured up by Art, in this sacred movie silence, somebody began to wind up his wrist watch, up, up, up, *without mercy*!!!- - - - - Too late.

Deo gratias

'We cannot be put into words and that is what we are putting into words. In which case art alone can assist in the universal lie. Besides, it's got to *insist* upon its ludicrous attempt *to put things into words* . . . To trust innocently in words, in putting things into words, is more than blind stupidity. It is a sin. But to renounce it, to scream bloody hell is at least as bad, because it leads to the creation of *voids*, yawning voids that might be filled in by the devil only knows what. To destroy and to assert, to spit and to talk. But how are we to talk when we have been left to fend for ourselves? When there is no God?

In the absence of God a Mass becomes horrible, merciless, awesome and perverse. The gnome Jesus as he step-dances in his spats on the stage of the world, or sits on his throne in the place of the Supreme Judge with no sky overhead, his chubby hands shaking, gazing at us, his people, with glassy eyes, burping as we chew gum like a pro.'

The lecturer

As soon as he walked into the cultural centre he bumped into a girl. She was pale and skinny. He said hello. The girl said nothing. She kept her lips tightly shut. She gave him a look of such utter despair you'd have thought she knew him. He was taken aback. 'What's the matter?' he asked at length. The girl was fighting something back, possibly her tears, possibly some old memory he had reawakened.

Then he saw the *salami* sandwich in the girl's hand, clutched tight against her skirt, with a piece of green pepper hanging out of it, like a tongue after a bad stomachache. 'Eating?' he asked like a schoolteacher. The girl nodded and swallowed. She was angry. They continued standing there without speaking. Someone poked his head timidly through a distant door.

'Why don't you eat it, for God's sake?!' he heard himself say. The girl turned away and began chomping her food. 'Thanks,' she said over her shoulder. Her mouth was full.

I

He staggered out of the smoke-filled club in the basement. He was not drunk, just in one hell of a rotten mood. He was living in a daze; it felt like some illness, or as if he'd been skinned alive. But he knew the cause of his illness, the shame he felt because of himself, coupled with the fear of others. Of others – the same society he held in contempt. Besides, the woman had a *bottomless pit* of invention. (Once, for instance: 'I love you. I still love you. So take pity on this woman who has been unfaithful – to herself.') Now she stepped up to him, it was night (he could see the moving chunks of billowing smoke) and he acted as if he were a stranger. 'I hate you, understand?' He nodded haughtily, two-thirty at night and a woman announces she hates him. Big deal. 'What do you want?' he asked coldly. She hated him because she *had* to read him, she said. 'Well,' he countered rather too sweetly, 'then don't. Love me. Don't read me.' At which his companion let out a triumphant laugh. 'If I don't read you, who is there to love?' Then, like a hired assassin, she disappeared.

I

He couldn't see anything in the dark except her arm, her bright, strong, lovely, brown, fleshy arm – a summer arm, he thought. When he dropped his hand in her lap hopelessly, as if he were still ill, the girl took it, a gesture like his mother's. He felt such a surge of gratitude well up in him, he'd have done anything she asked. But the time passed, and the girl asked for nothing. Her palm was still hot.

I

The gratitude and the terror, the fatigue and the emptiness he reserved for the following day. The woman, his Redeemer, was already at home. In short, there was something impersonal about it.

I

So many flies (by night)! I fly by night.

Triumph

A boy with chickenpox stepped up to him and said, 'Got off this time!' What got off or who got off he would not say.

His papa

'God bless papa,' he thought on his father's birthday. 'All things considered, his virtues are undying.' 'Hey, there, touslehead, where's your mama?'

His mama

He suddenly realised why his mother had hated spiders and why she was so *nervous* when, whispering words of endearment, he set them – especially the daddy-longlegs! – free. It was the web!

Simile

He knocked into someone. His ribs made a cracking sound and the pain, the pain refused to subside. It was a strange hide-and-seek sort of pain. Intangible. 'Well, what is it like?' the doctor asked, annoyed. He sighed, though not out of self-pity this time, but because he was attempting to localise the pain. 'As if I were very sad,' he said. They found no visible sign of bone fracture.

The outcome of the game

There is also that subdued, humdrum and obstinate happiness
you feel when a game which is rapidly losing its zest unexpectedly
ends in victory.

The eunuch of life

You can't be careful enough, he thought, a cold hatred is liable
to spring up in you under the most unexpected and innocent
circumstances. For instance, we might be holding a colour magazine which instructs us on the ideal way to season beef and
reveals some clever tricks to turn our utterly useless attic into an
exciting place by the efficacious use of large wooden beams. We
then quickly skip over the dress patterns until our eye is arrested
by the deceptive loveliness of some 'easily attainable' holiday
spot. And though we are not deceived by the flirty little miss
smiling in the appropriate corner of the photo – still, it can
happen.

The weakling

When his splitting headache had gone into its third day, which
made him think time and again of Eternity (while, practically
speaking, he hated himself), he clasped his hands. 'Fine. You
win. Ask anything you want, Lord, and you shall have it.' How
childish, cowardly and impudent!

History

On the loggia we liked to call the terrace, we kept a rabbit. Above
the city, so the annals say, there appeared an imperial eagle
without war insignia, and with a terrifying screech swooped down

on our poor rabbit, tearing it to bloody bits, pulling the skin off its head. (Oh, God, it's not true, the truth was worse, much worse! It was a Russian polecat, a polecat, a polecat.)

Naval base

When during a discussion he harped on the theoretically significant comment (or so it seemed to him) that not only the Hungarians ... that not only they ... that others in Transylvania had problems (and joys), too, they looked at him as if he were a moron, a traitorous moron[36] who had it so good at home he'd lost his better judgement. 'Have you ever lived there?' a woman asked. He saw she was attractive. He shook his head. 'So what makes you think you know?' From then on, no one would give him the time of day.

He could understand them. He even accepted their feelings. But he also knew that truth was on his side.

The long goodbye

When he took his aunt to the railroad station he ran into a college student, a distant acquaintance. It was hot, sweltering hot, as they say. The sky lay over the city like some bad, hot baking tin, while the sun was eclipsed by the type of clouds that in official weather reports are usually referred to as cirro-stratus or veil-clouds.

His aunt did not live with them at the time, which always made

---

[36] Graffiti on a Franklin statue in New York: 'Fuck your patriotism!'

their meetings highly intense. The train had already pulled out, and he was standing around with his hands stuck in his pockets. The skin of the people around him was shiny and sticky. He tried to conjure up his aunt's countenance. It worked. 'I hate goodbyes,' his aunt had said while he swung back and forth on the steps. 'Take care of yourself.' His aunt smiled. Sometimes her whole being would open up all the way, and then he would feel that the large space where he was *floating* or whatever, it was for him only, and that it was *good*; at other times she would close up grimly, as if she were ashamed of what had just transpired. At such times he was like a grown-up, he wouldn't look her in the eye, but would timidly hang his head. The loudspeaker was repeating the usual sentence: 'Kanizsa track 9, three minutes.' His aunt burst out. 'Will you listen to that sentence!' He laughed and resumed swinging on the step. He was just a young man of twenty-six at the time. 'Tell me. What kind of a world is it that can produce such sentences! (Later – now – when he remembers, sentences like this fill his heart with a sense of hatred and bewilderment.)

Hysterical, perspiring, overburdened mothers were dragging their nasty little offspring behind them as if their lives depended on . . . well, never mind. He was always taken aback, finding it difficult to believe his eyes whenever he saw certain husbands cling to their beautiful wives. Within five (!) minutes he'd seen two such couples, and both men hurled *the same reproach* at their wives: they should have ordered a taxi in advance. The first woman walked away without a word. The second turned and hissed, 'Just get off my back, okay?' The women could have passed for sisters – wide skirts, a dancer's legs, wide-brimmed hats.

The emptiness inside was tugging at him. The young man said hello. At first he didn't know who he was. 'Do I know you?' he asked grudgingly, and the young man said that they were distantly acquainted. He was waiting for someone his father would be operating on the next day. He found this touching and decided that the young man must have a kind heart. They talked, especially about French novels; he liked to talk about 19th-century French novels even back then. He wanted to get away. The young man said a noncommittal but polite goodbye. He also said that they would surely meet again some day at some other station. For his part, he nodded haughtily and left. It was like something out of a not too awful grade-B picture, towards the end.

Outside, as he passed the phone booths, it hit him how he might possibly never see the boy again, ever. He panicked. He was not prepared for such a serious eventuality. He ran back, but could not find him. He knew his family name, so he began to make desperate calls from one of the booths, from time to time rushing over to the nearby flowerstand for change. It cost just one forint back then. Meanwhile, he got entangled in the most incredible adventures. For instance, a man told him that he'd met a nympho-maniac the other day who wouldn't let him go until he bailed himself out through the services of a friend; a woman had her fridge stolen, and he thought that was why she was on the phone; the woman suspected a certain Lajos, who was using and humiliating her in a despicable manner, but she wouldn't want to leave him, she said, because of the difference in their ages, which puts her *ahead*, considering, but the fridge is going too far, she can't be expected to drink lukewarm beer in this weather.

Many others things happened, besides, but the boy he could not find. He felt that he had aged and was no longer twenty-six, but thirty-two.

Infuriated, he went up to a woman with a wiggly behind. 'Need help?' he asked. 'Help?' the woman said casually. He shrugged. 'Get lost,' the woman said. He did. A woman past her prime but apparently well to do gave him a yearning look. He smiled wickedly. Feeling impudent, he grabbed her boob while with his free hand he showed the girl's boyfriend the way to the metro. He gave change to an elderly lady, saw her to the coffee automat, then tripped her up. He apologised, helped her to her feet and pinched her withered arm so it hurt, then gave her his remaining change. He ended up with a whore who had a bad face, but no, her face was friendly enough, just pockmarked. She glanced calmly at him, which calmed him, too. He walked side by side not knowing how he should touch her, because he didn't want to touch her the way he usually did. Besides, he had no strength left to act superior. He gave her a sidelong glance. Her figure was tolerable, muscular, yet everything out of proportion, *exaggerated*.

The coyote

The friend who was in trouble, still the same trouble, called him. For a while they skirted the issue, talking about ostensibly important literary matters instead, Babits, György Rónay, the vacuum in a life of literature, the lack of self-determination, the importance of the past, of tradition, the present, and then, approaching by degrees, about what refined and tactful word there was for when criticism – *not now, of course, but in the past* – would bring devastation to its subject, smashing everything around it, crash-bang, everything within reach, by labelling it existentialist, volksbundist and homosexual. At such times the critics lack generosity of heart, yes, that was it, *generosity.* They were still ingeniously keeping time at bay. Today you got *generosity* of all types, from Twiggy to Marilyn, now there's generosity of proportion for you, in whose shade – indeed, valley! – every man can find a home; but truth to tell, the situation is more *varied* than peachy, seeing how most of the bosoms are padded, usually with rolls, which from a distance impart the appearance of youth and firmness, i.e., of reality, but if we touch them, which experience tells us is bound to happen sooner or later, they begin to crumble. That's what rolls are like. And most embarrassing of all, they laughed, is the crumbs. The way the *boobs crumble.*

Then they touched upon the problem after all, and the picture they were painting was turning darker by the minute. Then he thought of a simile, and this raised his spirits. He told his friend. His friend said nothing. Truth to tell, he found the suggestion rather too simple and optimistic himself. 'So then, we are standing at the mouth of a *new, dark* tunnel.' His friend said he didn't get it, it was too abstract. He had suspected as much himself, though he had meant it in a more *concrete way,* except being a coyote with no spunk, he was afraid to say so.

A thousand years

He saw a big, slothful man with a huge ass and thighs like hams, but as he began to speak his body was transformed into something pleasant, melodious, refined. He watched this wondrous transformation with pleasure. Another man's gesture, the supercilious movement of his lips, was like one of his very old friend's, so he felt as if he'd known this man, too, for a thousand years. Thus, though he had nothing whatsoever to do with him, he loved him.

Strindberg

During an indistinct phase of an overcomplicated entanglement which was uncertainty in the flesh, and in which neither party knew anything for certain any more, who he or she was, who the other, what one's own interests were and whether at any given moment one was concretely feeling love or hate, assuming that these are really so very different, and where hope is the name given to the minuscule left-over margin where change is still possible, where certain steps can still be taken for better or for worse, sometimes mutually humiliating, sometimes mutually respectful, but more like the former, in short, it was real hope after all, even if not quite a *ray* of hope, the terrain where each could almost think that neither had anything left, nothing intact where he or she could have retreated with nothing left but his own filth – at this juncture one of the two would say, 'I am not angry. But what's the use of explaining the Ninth Symphony to the *deaf*? Not that it's anybody's fault.' He propped himself up on the lounge chair. 'Unless that anybody happens to be Beethoven.' Time and again he caught himself sitting leaning on his hand, absent-mindedly listening to the ringing chorus of balm-crickets chirping in the sleepy pine groves under the sweltering sky.

In the eye of the storm

Nothing but negative elements throughout, betrayal, bitterness, lies, lies, 'and then', at the end, the camera stirs, a shaft of light breaks through the foliage, two people bow to each other, one word, and again the word, hit, hit, hit! (Hit parade.)

Lies

He often flattered himself in all sincerity that just like everybody else he also had ten thousand souls,[37] and that he was leading a double life at the very least. That's what he called his lies.

That he had no substance, no conscience, just nerves, grains of sand in the wind, that he didn't even exist. That's what he called his lies.

He had many names for his lies. But the woman he still loved with all his heart.

The mother

I dreamt I kissed you on your deathbed, my son. Your mouth caved in, like the mouths of old women and old graves, and you wheezed each time you inhaled. When I kissed you with a light kiss the wheezing grew stronger, suddenly you began to gasp for air, and a caterpillar, thick as my arm, wormed its way out of your mouth. *This big.* The caterpillar had a large, light-green head, the same colour as the faded cover of Győző Határ's Sterne translation in the 1955 edition, and it laughed like that cabaret artist, you know the one, his name escapes me now of course.

A laughing green caterpillar, *what next, son*, oh, I felt so ashamed.

[37] A puny little Faust, his own Mephisto.

The novel

In short, he decided, the hero is the one who stands by the side
of the road watching the never-ending string of passing cars and
coolly, painfully, with resignation and terror, and a little joyfully,
too, asks, '*How long can this go on?*' Our Yevgenin just stands
there lightning-struck, trembling.

Defeat

Spring was coming. He took careful note that spring was coming.
Which made him highly elated, as if it were his own doing. *As if
he were responsible for spring.*

'Pourquoi écrivez vous?'

Why do we write?

'We all have our reasons. For some of us art means flight, for
others it is a means of conquest. But one can flee into seclusion,
into madness or death, and it is possible to advance at gun-point.
Why does anyone choose *writing*, then, as a means of flight or
conquest?' I read. I read: 'We write so they will love us, and they
read us in a way that excludes their loving us. In all probability
it is this distance that makes the writer.'

Because, what is the prose-writer like today? He is like a swan.
Today, most swans in Europe are bred under semi-wild conditions. The singing swan nests on the shores of the seas, lakes,
rivers, or swamps. It feeds on plants. It is a protected species.
Swans come to Hungary individually or in small groups.

In short, I write for pleasure, out of fear, for freedom and out of freedom, because 'I have no love for this intoxicating, loathsome and maddening world and I am bent on changing it,' *zitat ende*, I write.

Notes by the author

The notes and comments that follow will not make this book easier to understand, but perhaps they will make it easier *to guess at*. After all, what is reading if not the process of rediscovering a book time and time and again?

Introduction to Literature – an ambitious project by the author (1978–1985). Books that together comprise a whole. The title of this approximately 700–page work is *Introduction to Literature*. The title also reflects the author's knowledge of mathematics, *cf.*, *Introduction to Geometry*. The genre: a book. The books that make up its parts are also whole to the extent that they cannot count on help from each other. Of the series *The Helping Verbs of the Heart* is available in English.

Trabant, Pobyeda, Chaika – <u>Trabant</u>: the East-German wonder-car made out of cardboard. With tail-winds and going downhill it can reach a dizzying speed of up to 100 km/hr, while its engine accomplishes in just two strokes what a Mercedes or BMW needs four strokes to do. Which is yet another proof of the superiority of socialism. With just a little exaggeration we might regard the Trabant as the symbol of Kádár's 'goulash socialism'.

The <u>Pobyeda</u> and <u>Chaika</u> were automobiles of the Soviet fifties.

The former would have been a kind of Volkswagen of the people if only the people had cars; the latter was the automobile of the authorities, who, unlike the common folk, had more than enough cars to go around. (Which they did, especially in the wee hours of the morning. When Hungarians say that they were afraid of every knock on the door, they were *really* afraid of every knock on the door.)

HÓDIKÖT – acronym for the Hódmezővásárhely Textile Works (Hódmezövásárhelyi Kötöttárúgyár). Hódmezővásárhely is a town in south-eastern Hungary. Though the author was in the army there in 1969, this has nothing to do with the book (unless you think of it as a reluctant homage), while textile works are textile works any way you look at it. The times gave rise to many such mosaic-words. There was something frightening about them. They had meaning, and they did not. The way political structure sneaks inside a language is loaded with frightful implications.

The question of quotes – a difficult question. The author quotes frequently and without supplying his source from the likes of Defoe through contemporary Hungarian newspapers and Wittgenstein (the closing sentences of the scenes of Part I, written in an adulterated language). The author also quotes from his own works, especially in Part IV. His intention is not for the reader to recognise any of these quotes but to create the tension that the introduction of a foreign text (body) will precipitate.

The author borrows not only sentences but finished forms as well. One example is the anecdote form used in Part II. The original anecdotes come from an anthology about customs officials from the turn of the century, a period we like to refer to as 'the good old times' or 'the peace years'. It was into these triumphant and quaint stories of life in the Austro–Hungarian Empire that the author chose to insert the terrifying words of a specific dictatorship (this is how Emperor Francis Joseph became Comrade Rákosi) to see how they would act upon each other. There were those who, for moral reasons, objected to this (*cf. Consolidation*).

Part III owes a debt of gratitude to *The Hite Report* (a 'comprehensive study of female sexuality' in which '3,019 women between the ages of 14 and 78 talk about their most intimate concerns'); the questionnaires and sexual concepts and ways of talking about sex found in this book have been transcribed and transferred to the political and societal spheres (*ex:* lovemaking = bloody battle, orgasm = democratic experience, masturbation = self-delusion, lesbianism = internecine warfare, woman = Kurucz; man = Labancz, and so on). Which is as good a place as any to say a few words about the *Kurucz* and the *Labancz*, inconceivable except as a pair (Laurel and Hardy, Keats and Shelley). Put simply, they were originally the participants of the Rákóczi freedom fights (1703–1711) involving the poor folk (the Kurucz) in a popular uprising against the House of Habsburg and those who sided with them, including many a Hungarian. The Kurucz is the good guy, the Labancz the traitor, or the bad guy. The author's family (see Haydn) is eminently Labancz, though being a *populous* family, it has a number of Kurucz among its ranks. In more recent times the Kurucz would be the nation-loving anti-communist, the Labancz the communist-sympathiser and henchman.

Summing up what has been said about quotations, if you find an especially clever sentence in the book, the chances are better than even that it is quote. If it is clever but you don't know what it means, it is from Wittgenstein.

King Mátyás – the illustrious 15th-century monarch who brought the Renaissance to Hungary, and incidentally stopped the Turkish onslaught from the east while he was alive. According to one view, which the author does not share, after Mátyás's death Hungarian history has been nothing but a series of *oys, veys*, lamentations and defeats.

There are many stories and anecdotes about 'Mátyás the Just', who went about the country in disguise punishing the bad and rewarding the good. As you can see, the author has made unabashed use of him, since it just so happens that Rákosi's first name was also Mátyás, while his last name *almost* sounds like Rákóczi of freedom-fight fame (see above).

Mátyás Rákosi (1892–1956?), said to be one of Stalin's best pupils, was Hungary's very own Stalin, 'the chief perpetrator of the dogmatic and sectarian errors that proliferated after 1949' (*New Hungarian Lexicon*). As First Secretary of the Hungary Communist Party, he was the country's 'king'. When the 1956 popular uprising 'dethroned' him, he was whisked away to Moscow, which is the last anyone knows about him for certain.

Gerő, Révai, Farkas – the Triumvirate in Mátyás Rákosi's closest retinue.

<u>Ernő Gerő</u> (1898–1956) – first Minister of Transport, then Minister of Finance and Minister of Foreign Affairs, respectively, 'he had a major hand in the initial triumphs of the people's democracy, but after the proletariat came to power, he and Rákosi committed some grievous errors in the course of building socialism' (*New Hungarian Lexicon*). Asking Déry for his advise was one (*cf. The solution*).

<u>József Révai</u> (1898–1959) – founding member of the Hungarian Communist Party, and from 1945 to 1950 editor in chief of the Party daily *Szabad Nép*, which figures in our story (see pp. 48). In his free hours, also member of the Party's Central Committee and Minister of Culture. Consequently, may I not see him in my worst dreams!

<u>Mihály Farkas</u> – like Wittgenstein (see footnote 5), never once mentioned in the *New Hungarian Lexicon*. Minister of Defence under Rákosi, he was Rákosi's right hand and most probably the man really in charge of the *ÁVÓ*, the infamous secret police (which is why he's not mentioned in the *New Hungarian Lexicon*). The ÁVÓ was to Hungary what the KGB was to the Soviet Union. Its headquarters, along with a gaol and torture chambers, were located in a beautiful *fin de siècle* building at Andrássy út 60, Budapest's most luxurious boulevard. People still get the shivers when they walk past. Hand in hand, Rákosi, just back from Moscow (!), Gerő, Révai and Farkas, did a neat job of imposing the Stalinist political model on Hungary. However, the presence of the Soviet army helped.

Rákosi was followed by *János Kádár* (1923–1989), who as First Secretary of the Party first did away with those who were involved in the 1956 'anti-revolutionary' (read 'anti-Soviet') uprising, then loosened the reins. By the eighties Kádár was credited with cooking up a 'Communism with a human face', also known as 'velvet Communism'. He also introduced small-time or 'goulash' capitalism. He conveniently died just a few months before the free elections of 1989.

The Horthy regime – the governor of Hungary between the two world wars was one Miklós Horthy, whose main claim to fame, as far as I'm concerned, is that as a young man he was supposed to have learned English from Joyce. The Horthy regime was nothing to write home about, but it was not quite fascist either. To quote the eminent Hungarian historian István Bibó, 'at its inception and decline it was a semi-fascist regime, while in the interim period, during the consolidation, it was a conservative police state'.

16th of June – a good example of literary literature clashing with Central-European reality. 'A brutalised culture,' as Gombrowicz called it. It is also a good example of how collusion between the lines works – *i.e.*, saying something without *actually* saying it.

1. Bloosmday: since Joyce's *Ulysses*, every novel takes place on this day.

2. Imre Nagy, the leading figure of the 1956 popular uprising against communist rule, was executed by the Kádár government on the 16th of June 1958.